JAMES PATTERSON
BOOKSHOTS

Dear Reader,

You're about to experience a revolution in reading — BookShots.

BookShots are a whole new kind of book — 100 percent story-driven, no fluff, always under $5.

I've written or co-written nearly all the BookShots and they're among my best novels of any length.

At 150 pages or fewer, BookShots can be read in a night, on a commute, or even on your cell phone during breaks at work.

I hope you enjoy *Manhunt*.

James Patterson

P.S.

For special offers and the full list of BookShots titles, please go to **BookShots.com**

BOOK**SHOTS**

BOOKSHOTS
Flames

MANHUNT

A MICHAEL BENNETT STORY

JAMES PATTERSON
WITH JAMES O. BORN

BOOK**SHOTS**

Little, Brown and Company

New York Boston London

Copyright © 2017 JBP Business, LLC
Excerpt from *Ambush* copyright © 2018 by James Patterson

Hachette Book Group supports the right to free expression and the value of copyright. The purpose of copyright is to encourage writers and artists to produce the creative works that enrich our culture.

The scanning, uploading, and distribution of this book without permission is a theft of the author's intellectual property. If you would like permission to use material from the book (other than for review purposes), please contact permissions@hbgusa.com. Thank you for your support of the author's rights.

BookShots / Little, Brown and Company
Hachette Book Group
1290 Avenue of the Americas, New York, NY 10104
bookshots.com

First Edition: November 2017

BookShots is an imprint of Little, Brown and Company, a division of Hachette Book Group, Inc. The Little, Brown name and logo are trademarks of Hachette Book Group, Inc. The BookShots name and logo are trademarks of JBP Business, LLC.

The publisher is not responsible for websites (or their content) that are not owned by the publisher.

The Hachette Speakers Bureau provides a wide range of authors for speaking events. To find out more, go to hachettespeakersbureau.com or call (866) 376-6591.

ISBN 978-0-316-47349-1
LCCN 2017938657

10 9 8 7 6 5 4 3 2

LSC-C

Printed in the United States of America

MANHUNT

CHAPTER 1

MY ENTIRE BROOD, plus Mary Catherine and my grandfather, gathered in the living room. We'd been told to expect a call from Brian between eight and eight fifteen. That gave us enough time to eat, clean up, and at least start the mountain of homework that nine kids get from one of the better Catholic schools in New York City.

We had the phone set on speaker and placed it in the middle of the group, which was getting a little antsy waiting for the call.

At exactly ten minutes after eight, the phone rang and some dull-voiced New York Department of Corrections bureaucrat told us that the call would last approximately ten minutes and that it would be monitored. Great.

My oldest son, Brian, had made a mistake. A big mistake—selling drugs. Now he was paying for that mistake, and so were we.

Tonight was Thanksgiving eve. Tomorrow we would embark on our annual tradition of viewing the Macy's Thanksgiving Day Parade, and it would hurt not having Brian with us.

My late wife and I had begun this tradition even before we started adopting kids. She'd get off her shift at the hospital and

I'd meet her near Rockefeller Center. When the kids were little, she loved the parade more than they did. It was one of many traditions I kept alive to honor her memory.

She even made the parade after chemo had wrecked her body, with a scarf wrapped around her head. The beauty still managed an excited smile at the sight of Bart Simpson or Snoopy floating by.

As soon as Brian came on the line, there was a ripple in our crowd. The last time I'd seen him, he was still recovering from a knife attack that was meant to send me a message.

Tonight, he sounded good. His voice was clear and still had that element of the kid to it. No parent can ever think of their child as a convicted felon, even if he's sitting in a prison. Currently, Brian was temporarily housed at Bear Hill Correctional, in the town of Malone, in northern New York. It was considered safe. For now. Mary Catherine and I talked over each other while we asked him about the dorm and classes.

Brian said, "Well, I can't start classes because I haven't been officially designated at a specific prison. That will happen soon."

All three of the boys spoke as a group. As usual, they took a few minutes to catch Brian up on sports. Football always seemed to be the same—the Jets look bad, the Patriots look good.

Then an interruption in the programming.

Chrissy, my youngest, started to cry. *Wail* is probably more accurate.

Mary Catherine immediately dropped to one knee and slipped an arm around the little girl's shoulder.

Chrissy moaned, "I miss Brian." She turned to the phone like there was a video feed and repeated, "I miss you, Brian. I want you to come home."

There was a pause on the phone, then Brian's voice came through a little shakier. I could tell he was holding back tears by the way he spoke, haltingly. "I can't come home right now, Chrissy, but you can do something for me."

"Okay."

"Go to the parade tomorrow and have fun. I mean, so much fun you can't stand it. Then I want you to write me a letter about it and send it to me. Can you do that?"

Chrissy sniffled. "Yes. Yes, I can."

I felt a tear run down my cheek. I have some great kids. I don't care what kind of mistakes they might've made.

We were ready for our adventure.

CHAPTER 2

IT WAS A bright, cloudless day and Mary Catherine had bundled the kids up like we lived at the North Pole. It was cold, with a decent breeze, but not what most New Yorkers would consider brutal. My grandfather, Seamus, would call it "crisp." It was too crisp for the old priest. He was snuggled comfortably in his quarters at Holy Name.

I wore an insulated Giants windbreaker and jeans. I admit, I looked at the kids occasionally and wished Mary Catherine had dressed me as well, but it wasn't that bad.

I herded the whole group to our usual spot, across from Rockefeller Center at 49th Street and Sixth Avenue. It was a good spot, where we could see all the floats and make our escape afterward with relatively little hassle.

I was afraid this might be the year that some of the older kids decided they'd rather sleep in than get up before dawn to make our way to Midtown. Maybe it was due to Chrissy's tearful conversation with Brian, but everyone was up and appeared excited despite the early hour.

Now we had staked out our spot for the parade, and were

waiting for the floats. It was perfect outside and I gave in to the overwhelming urge to lean over and kiss Mary Catherine.

Chrissy and Shawna crouched in close to us as Jane flirted with a couple of boys from Nebraska—after I'd spoken to them, of course. They were nice young men, in their first year at UN Kearney.

We could tell by the reaction of the crowd that the parade was coming our way. We sat through the first couple of marching bands and earthbound floats before we saw one of the stars of the parade: Snoopy, in his red scarf, ready for the Red Baron.

Of course, Eddie had the facts on the real Red Baron. He said, "You know, he was an ace in World War I for Germany. His name was Manfred von Richthofen. He had over eighty kills in dogfights."

The kids tended to tune out some of Eddie's trivia, but Mary Catherine and I showed interest in what he said. It was important to keep a brain like that fully engaged.

Like any NYPD officer, on or off duty, I keep my eyes open and always know where the nearest uniformed patrol officer is. Today I noticed a tall, young African American officer trying to politely corral people in our area, who ignored him and crept onto the street for a better photo.

I smiled, knowing how hard it is to get people to follow any kind of rules unless there is an immediate threat of arrest.

Then I heard it.

At first, I thought it was a garbage truck banging a dumpster as it emptied it. Then an engine revved down 49th Street, and I turned to look.

I barely had any time to react. A white Ford step-van truck barreled down the street directly toward us. It was gaining speed, though it must have had to slow down to get by the dump truck parked at the intersection of 49th and Sixth as a blockade.

Shawna was ten feet to my right, focused on Snoopy. She was directly in the path of the truck.

It was like I'd been shocked with electricity. I jumped from my spot and scooped up Shawna a split second before the truck rolled past us. I heard Mary Catherine shriek as I tumbled, with Shawna, on the far side of the truck.

The truck slammed into spectators just in front of us. One of the boys from Nebraska bounced off the hood with a sickening thud. He lay in a twisted heap on the rough asphalt. His University of Nebraska jacket was sprayed with a darker shade of red as blood poured from his mouth and ears.

The truck rolled onto the parade route until it collided with a sponsor vehicle splattered with a Kellogg's logo. The impact sent a young woman in a purple pageant dress flying from the car and under the wheels of a float.

Screams started to rise around me, but I couldn't take my eyes off the truck.

The driver made an agile exit from the crumpled driver's door and stood right next to the truck. Over his face, he wore a red scarf with white starburst designs.

He shouted, *"Hawqala!"*

CHAPTER 3

I STOOD IN shock like just about everyone else near me. This was not something we were used to seeing on US soil.

Eddie and Jane, crouching on the sidewalk next to me, both stood and started to move away from me.

I grabbed Eddie's wrist.

He looked back at me and said, "We've got to help them."

Jane had paused right next to him as I said, "We don't know what's going to happen."

As I said it, the driver of the truck reached in his front jacket pocket and pulled something out. I couldn't identify it exactly, but I knew it was a detonator.

I shouted as loud as I could, "Everyone down!" My family knew to lie flat on the sidewalk and cover their faces with their hands. A few people in the crowd listened to me as well. Most were still in shock or sobbing.

The driver hit the button on the detonator and immediately there was a blinding flash, and what sounded like a thunderclap echoed among all the buildings.

I couldn't turn away as I watched from the pavement. The

blast blew the roof of the truck straight into the air almost thirty feet. I felt it in my guts. A fireball rose from the truck.

The driver was dazed and stumbled away from the truck as the roof landed on the asphalt not far from him.

Now there was absolute pandemonium. It felt like every person on 49th Street was screaming. The blast had rocked the whole block.

The parade was coming to an abrupt stop. Parade vehicles bumped one another and the marching band behind the step van scattered. A teenager with a trumpet darted past me, looking for safety.

The driver pushed past spectators on the sidewalk near us and started to run back down 49th Street where he had driven the truck.

The ball of flame was still rising like one of the floats. Then I noticed a couple of the floats were rising in the air as well. The human anchors had followed instinct and run for their lives.

Snoopy was seventy-five feet in the air now.

Several Christmas tree ornaments as big as Volkswagens, with only three ropes apiece, made a colorful design as they passed the middle stories of Rockefeller Center.

I glanced around, but didn't see any uniformed cops close. The one young patrolman I had seen keeping people in place was frantically trying to help a child who had been struck by the truck.

I had no radio to call for backup. I just had my badge and my off-duty pistol hidden in my waistband.

There had been plenty of cops early, but now I saw that some of them had been hurt in the explosion, others were trying to help victims. It was mayhem, and no one was chasing the perp. I was it. I had to do something.

CHAPTER 4

WHEN I STOOD up, my legs still a little shaky, I concentrated on the red scarf I'd seen around the driver's face and neck as he fled the scene. The splash of color gave me something to focus on.

I looked around at my family, making sure everyone was still in one piece. They were on the ground and I said, "Stay put."

I worked my way past panicked parade spectators until I was in the open street and could see the driver half a block ahead. I broke into a sprint, dodging tourists like a running back.

By this point, no one realized the man running from the scene was the driver. The people this far back on the street didn't have a front row seat to the tragedy. No one tried to stop him. Everyone was scrambling for safety, if there was such a place.

I started to gain on the man because he hadn't realized yet that he was being pursued. He had a loping gait as if one of his legs was injured. But he was also alert, checking each side and behind him as he hurried away.

I wasn't a rookie chasing my first purse-snatcher in the Bronx. I didn't feel the urge to yell, "Stop—police!" I was silent and hung back a little bit so he didn't pick up on me.

He took the corner, then slowed. He looked around, as if he was expecting someone to meet him. I paused at the edge of a high-end fashion boutique and watched him for a moment. I still hadn't drawn my pistol, to avoid attracting attention.

Finally, the truck driver decided his ride wasn't here and started down the street again. He looked over his shoulder one time as he approached a packed diner, and surprised me by slipping inside.

I looked in the window as I came to the door of the diner. Every patron and server was glued to the TV in the corner of the room. News of the attack was mesmerizing. The room was silent as the news had just broken—the same TV parade footage was on loop as the newscaster started repeating the information he was receiving. No conversation, no clinking of silverware, nothing.

I immediately stepped to the cashier by the front door, held up my badge, and said in a low voice, "NYPD. Did you see where the man who just came in here went?"

The dark-haired young woman shook her head. She mumbled, "I didn't notice anyone." Then she turned and looked back at the TV.

Even though the attack had happened only a couple blocks away, a few minutes ago, watching it on TV made it feel like it was in another country.

I saw the hallway that led past the kitchen. There was a sign that said RESTROOM, so I presumed a back door was that way as well. So I hustled, squeezing past several tables crowded with extra patrons. Today was a big day for New York eateries.

Just as I started to pick up my pace, I heard something behind me and turned. The man I'd been chasing was lowering himself from an awkward position above the door. What the hell? It looked like it was out of the movies.

When he dropped to the floor and faced me, I realized he had led me into a trap.

CHAPTER 5

THE TRUCK DRIVER and I stared at each other for a moment. He had taken off the scarf, having used it to trick me. Pretty sharp.

He was about thirty, with neat, dark hair and blue eyes.

I reached for my pistol.

He reacted instantly and blocked my arm. That was from training. That's not a natural move. Then he head-butted me. Hard. My brain rattled and vision blurred.

I stumbled back and kept reaching for my pistol. Just as I pulled it from under my Giants windbreaker, the man swatted it out of my hand. I heard it clatter onto the hard, wooden floor— then the man kicked it.

The gun spun as it slid across the floor and under a radiator.

The man nodded to me and sprinted away. He didn't want to fight, he just wanted to escape.

I couldn't let that happen.

I was dazed and unable to reach my pistol, but I had to do something. I just put one foot in front of the other and followed the man.

My head started to clear.

A moment later, I found myself in the kitchen. The cooks and busboys weren't paying any attention to us. They were watching the news, just like everyone else, but on one of their smartphones. The back door wasn't at the end of the hall, like I had expected, but through the kitchen.

The man was almost to the back door when he turned and saw me. He looked annoyed, and he turned his full attention on me and charged forward.

I picked up a bottle of cooking wine and smashed it across his face just before he reached me.

The driver teetered back. Blood poured out of a gash on his cheek. Just as I was about to subdue him so I could call for backup, his foot flew up and connected with my chin.

That was the second time this asshole had made me see stars.

This time he took the opportunity and ran. He was out the door in a flash.

CHAPTER 6

IT TOOK A minute to get my legs under me. One of the cooks made the connection between the events at the parade and the fight in his kitchen. He helped me stumble out onto the street, but I saw no sign of the terrorist. He had fled back into the chaos he'd created and there was no telling where he was headed.

After retrieving my gun, I'd made my first phone call to dispatch, telling them where I was and what had happened. Now I was talking to a heavyset patrol sergeant and two Intel detectives.

Tom Colgan, the senior Intel guy, had been raised in Queens and now lived on Long Island. I'd known him for too long. We had a lot in common. He was from a classic Irish Catholic family and had four kids of his own.

Now he said, "So after this guy kicked your ass, he just disappeared into the crowd."

I nodded. He had summed it up pretty well. Then I remembered when the truck plowed into the crowd and said, "He yelled something before he detonated the bomb in the truck. I didn't recognize it."

Colgan said, "Allahu Akbar?"

"No. I've heard that before. Frankly, I almost expected him to say that. But this was different."

Colgan said, "They're rounding up all the witnesses now. I'm sure more than a few people caught the whole thing on video." He paused for a minute, then said, "Your family is okay, right?"

"They're coming to meet me here in a little while."

Colgan said, "I'm not kidding when I say I'm surprised someone was able to fight you off, then flee."

"What can I say? The guy had skills." I looked over and saw that Colgan had taken several pages of notes, including the description I'd already given him. The NYPD Intel detectives were some of the sharpest people I'd ever met. He had more information on two sheets of paper already than I take down on a whole case sometimes.

The uniformed sergeant, clearly a Brooklyn native with a long Italian name, got on the radio and gave out the limited description I had of the driver. He was clear and thorough. That's exactly what we needed right now. A patrolman was going to drive me down to One Police Plaza to work with a sketch artist.

I could still hear sirens in the distance. Cops were everywhere. The parade was canceled, and everything in a two-block radius was closed off while the bomb squad made sure there were no other nasty surprises. It was complete mayhem.

This was not the Thanksgiving Day I had envisioned.

CHAPTER 7

I WAS TOGETHER with my family by the time darkness fell. Other than when I was at police headquarters, I had been on the phone just about all day with one person or another from the NYPD. There were several still photographs of the bomber holding the detonator where you could see the kids and me in the background. One photo had already appeared on CNN and ABC.

CNN had named the attack "Holiday Terror." The theme music had just a hint of Eastern influence. I wondered if that was intentional.

Even after seeing all the footage and the news that six were dead and twelve seriously injured, all I could think about was how much worse it could've been. I was standing there. I saw the crowds. Just the truck itself plowing into them could have killed twenty people, but the driver hadn't been able to get to full speed, because he'd had to slow down to get around the dump truck that was blocking off the intersection. Thank God.

The bomb itself caused very little damage. Mainly it ripped apart the truck. The blast didn't cause any additional injuries.

Had the explosive been set properly and the blast spread out in every direction, the result would've been very different. Just the idea of it made me shudder. More than one witness interviewed thought 'it was a miracle the exploding truck didn't kill many more.

Seamus said, "These people are taking it too lightly. It *was* miraculous. God *did* intervene."

Fiona looked at her great-grandfather and said, "Why didn't God stop the truck driver in the first place?" It was a simple question asked by an innocent girl, no trap or guile in it.

My grandfather turned and put his hand on Fiona's cheek. "Because, dear girl, God gave man free will. It's not something he can turn on and off."

Fiona said, "I learned about free will at CCD. Does it basically mean we are responsible for the things we do?"

Seamus said, "Exactly."

I noticed Trent frantically searching something on his phone. Recently he had been making a concerted effort to match his brother Eddie's intellectual output. A tall task by any measure.

Trent said, "C. S. Lewis wrote, 'Free will, though it makes evil possible, is also the only thing that makes possible any love or goodness or joy worth having.'" He turned and gave me a sly smile.

I chuckled and said, "Good job, Trent. Watch out or you might end up studying philosophy."

Trent said, "Why do you say it like that? *You* studied philosophy."

I wanted to say, "Look where that got me." Instead, I just nodded and said, "And enjoyed every minute of it."

Finally, we gathered for our Thanksgiving dinner. When we were all around the long table, with one chair left empty for Brian, as had become our custom, we joined hands and Seamus said grace.

"Thank you, God, for this family being safe after what they witnessed. I can ask no more of you at this moment. The fact that we are all here together makes everything else in life trivial. We thank you for your guidance and understanding as we humans try to figure things out."

The old guy could still make his point in a quick and efficient way.

Later, as I was helping the kids clean off the table, my phone rang. I was prepared to let it go directly to voice mail, but I noticed it was from my lieutenant, Harry Grissom.

I tried to hide the weariness in my voice when I said, "Hey, Harry, how has your day been?" That got the rare laugh from my boss.

"You did a good job out there today."

"You mean except for the part where I let a suspect beat my ass and get away."

"From what I hear, you got a good look at him, you marked him with the cut on his face, and got a few licks of your own in. They all can't be home runs."

"Did you call just to try and cheer me up?"

"You're assigned to work with a joint terrorism task force at the FBI building starting tomorrow."

"Do they know that?"

"Frankly, I don't give a shit if the FBI wants to work with us. But we've gotta give it a chance. By pooling our resources, we have a better chance of catching this jerk-off and unrolling the cell he's connected with. And we gotta do it before they try something else."

CHAPTER 8

I WAS READY to go at six the next morning, but I had been told to arrive at the FBI building at eight o'clock sharp, so I enjoyed having a little extra time with the kids and Mary Catherine. But at eight, that's where I was: standing in front of the Jacob K. Javits Federal Building on the corner of Broadway and Worth Street in lower Manhattan.

The building was the standard, drab government off-white color with an efficient, if not attractive, design. There were low decorative posts all around the property to discourage car bombs.

I had friends here. Agents I'd worked with and analysts who had helped me solve some of my biggest cases. But the Bureau's attitude and ability to work with others was still questionable. Old habits die hard.

A tall, good-looking guy in his mid-thirties took his time coming down to collect me from the front desk. He stuck out a big hand and said, "Dan Santos. You must be Mike Bennett."

We walked slowly to a conference room behind the main FBI door. I was impressed that the entire office seemed to have shown up ready to work.

As we walked, Santos said, "I thought about joining the NYPD after I graduated from Hofstra."

"What changed your mind?"

"I wanted to make a real difference in the world."

I said, "I hear you. Guess I don't mind just collecting a fat city paycheck without doing anything." I could tell this was going to be a long special assignment.

The conference room was the new headquarters for the investigation into yesterday's bombing. I recognized a few of the agents and a couple of the NYPD Intel people who were also working the case.

Santos walked me over to a woman sitting at a table in the corner. I could tell she was making a complete assessment of me with her pale-blue eyes. Apparently, I didn't impress or disturb her, because she didn't say a word and looked back at a report she was reading.

Santos said, "NYPD Detective Michael Bennett, meet our liaison from the Russian Embassy, Darya Kuznetsova."

The woman extended her hand and said with almost no accent, "A pleasure to make your acquaintance."

Her blond hair muted her hard-edged look. She was athletic, with broad shoulders, and attractive in every sense of the word. But something about her told me I'd never want to tangle with her.

Not knowing what else to do, I sat at the long table next to her. I tried to make small talk, without much success. Finally, I came right to the point and said, "What's your job with the Russian Embassy?"

She turned that pretty face to me and said, "For now, I am the Russian liaison to this investigation."

"I realize that. What is your title at the embassy?"

"I am just an assistant to the ambassador. They thought it would be a good idea for me to work with you because of Russia's own issues with terrorists, and I might see or hear something that American police officers might overlook due to differing cultures."

I said, "Am I missing something? Why would Russian culture be important in this investigation?"

That's when Dan Santos said, "I think all your questions will be answered during our briefing. Believe me, we're going to need all the help we can get."

CHAPTER 9

SANTOS STOOD UP in front of the gathered agents and NYPD people to get everyone's attention. There were maybe twenty-five people in the room now. The tall agent looked confident as he straightened his blue tie and faced the crowd. Of course, few people got to run a case like this unless they were confident. It was a key element to getting people to do what you needed them to do.

Santos gave a recap of what had happened, but he didn't say anything I had not already heard or personally witnessed.

We had several videos taken from bystanders' phones that covered almost every angle of the attack. He played all the videos a few times, ending them all just as the truck came to an abrupt halt and the driver stepped out and yelled, *"Hawqala!"*

Santos said, "Based on our analysis and the attacker's accent, we believe he is a Russian speaker from Kazakhstan. To help us with language and context, we have Darya Kuznetsova, who will be working the investigation with us."

Suddenly the attacker's neat hair and blue eyes made more

sense. Perhaps even his training. This was a wrinkle I had not been expecting.

Santos continued. "The Russians have excellent contacts with the Kazakhstan Security Forces and have a shared interest in working with us to curb terrorism."

We watched another video and some of the aftermath, and then Santos broke us down into smaller groups and explained what everyone would be doing. One group was only following up with interviews of witnesses. Another was working with informants to see if anything was being talked about on the street. A third group, which included analysts, was scouring computer databanks to see if it could find information that might shed some light on the attack.

When Santos said, "Any questions?" I could see the annoyance in his eyes when I raised my hand. He said, "Go ahead, Bennett."

"What, exactly, does *hawqala* mean?"

"Literally it means, 'There is no power nor strength save by Allah.'"

"I've never heard it before. Is it common?"

"Not in attacks like this. We're looking into it." He looked around the room. "Anything else?"

Once again, I raised my hand.

Santos just looked at me.

"Is there some significance to *hawqala*? Could it mean he's after something else or representing a certain group?"

"As I said, we're looking into it." Then he quickly moved on and introduced Steve Barborini from the Bureau of Alcohol, Tobacco, Firearms, and Explosives.

The tall, lean ATF man stood and looked around the room. He didn't use notes when he spoke. That meant he knew what he was talking about and he was confident about his subject matter. I liked that.

The ATF agent said, "Obviously we're still processing the van, the explosive, and parts of the scene. It looks like the device was fairly simple. It contained a five-gallon paint jug with an explosive made up mostly of commercial Tannerite, which is a brand name for the most popular binary explosive on the market. We're not absolutely sure how many pounds were crammed into the paint jug, but we're guessing it was at least twenty."

One of the FBI agents raised her hand. "Where could they buy something like that? How is it legal?"

"Tannerite can be bought anywhere. Even on Amazon. There hasn't been any big move to curb it. It's legal because it's sold in two different packages. Unless the packages are mixed, they are not explosive. That's why it's called a *binary* explosive."

That seemed to satisfy the FBI agent as she made a few notes and nodded her head.

Barborini went on. "There were nuts and bolts taped around the paint jug. The idea is that the explosion should have dispersed the nuts and bolts like shrapnel in a wide circle around the explosion. What we believe happened was that the metal paint jug that was used did not have a secure lid. The detonator was a simple blasting cap on an electronic igniter. When the blasting cap went off and started the chain reaction in the Tannerite, it blew the top off the paint can and the power of the explosion went straight up. That's why the roof of the truck blew off so neatly. An explosion will travel the path of least resistance. That's what saved so many lives."

CHAPTER 10

AFTER ALMOST AN hour of briefing, I wondered if all we were going to do on this case was have meetings. This went against my instincts—to get out on the street and start talking to people. In my experience as a cop, that's what always broke open major cases. People talk. It doesn't matter where they're from or what their reasons are for committing a crime. People always talk.

I couldn't find out what they were saying if I was sitting in a conference room in Federal Plaza.

Dan Santos went through the last few things on his list, explaining how the scarf over the attacker's face had thwarted any efforts to use facial recognition to match the attacker with photographs in the intelligence databases.

Santos turned to me and said, "Turns out that Detective Bennett here is the only one who's seen the attacker's face." He held up the police artist's sketch of the man I'd described. "This is based on Detective Bennett's description. There's nothing unusual about him except possibly a cut on his left cheek."

Then I had to speak up. "There's no *possibly* about it. The man has a decent gash on his left cheek from a broken bottle across his face." I could still feel the heft of the bottle, suddenly going weightless as it broke against his face.

Santos continued. "We're covering the leads on the step-van truck—which was a rental—immigration, current gripes against the US government, and even city employees. The last group is because the dump truck at the intersection was too far to one side, allowing the attacker to slip past.

"I know we have a lot of different agencies working together, but there will be an FBI agent in each group. They will document everything you do, brief me, and handle evidence."

He closed his notebook and straightened up to glance around the room. "Are there any questions?" He shot a dirty look at me in an effort to keep me quiet.

As everyone broke into their small groups with different assignments, Dan Santos walked over to me and Darya and said, "I'm on your team. We'll be handling a lot of different things. But no matter what we do, neither of you are to run down any leads without me. Is that clearly understood?"

I was preparing a smartass answer when Darya said, "I sorry. My English not so good. Let's hope I make no mistake." She turned to me, winked, and shot me a little smile.

I was liking this Darya more and more.

CHAPTER 11

I FELT LIKE I'd found a kindred spirit in Darya Kuznetsova after she stood up to the FBI agent, Dan Santos. It wasn't just what she did, but how she did it—it was playful yet said, *Don't mess with me.*

That's why I was comfortable sitting down next to her away from everyone else in the corner of the conference room. She seemed pleased that I had chosen to speak with her. She gave me just a hint of a lovely smile, but her sharp eyes didn't miss anything.

She said, "Do you always carry two pistols? I thought the NYPD usually carried only one gun, their duty weapon on the right hip."

"I decided a backup .380 on my ankle was a good idea considering how tough this suspect was. How did you pick up on it?"

"You dragged your left leg ever so slightly and I noticed your ankle holster. Your duty weapon on your hip is obvious."

"You don't approve of guns?"

"On the contrary, it's smart. The Kazakhs tend to be of a

rougher sort than most Russians. It would be similar to someone being raised on the frontier in the Old West." She grasped my right hand and held it up to examine it. "Just like I could tell you were not raised on the frontier."

I gave her a smile, though she had subtly just called me a wimp. "New York City is its own kind of frontier."

Darya considered my comment for a moment and said, "Were you ever pressured to join a group and commit crimes?"

I thought about mentioning the Holy Name basketball team when I was a kid. We'd been a tough bunch, and on a dare I'd stolen a bag of M&M's from a grocery store on the corner. But that probably wasn't what she meant, so I didn't mention it. Besides, I had gone back the next day to give old man Rogers, who ran the place, money for the candy.

I changed the subject and said, "I know we talked about this, but how did you get this assignment?"

"Part of it was that I happened to be here in New York and my English is better than most Russians."

"Your English is better than most New Yorkers." It was satisfying that the comment earned a smile.

"I was raised in Maryland. My father was in the diplomatic corps in Washington, DC. Then I attended MIT on a student visa."

"What did you study?"

"Engineering. I still get to use it occasionally. What about you? Did you go to college?"

"Right here in New York. Manhattan College."

"What did you study?"

"Philosophy." That one earned a little bit of a smirk.

"Do you ever get to use your degree?"

"That depends. If my studies did, in fact, open my mind to help me better understand the human condition, then yes, I do. If I was merely sucked into the factory of higher education designed solely to make money, I still use it every day."

"What do you think we will be doing on this investigation? Will the FBI try to hinder us?"

"I guarantee the FBI will try to hinder us. Some of the NYPD Intel detectives say that the FBI stands for *Forever Being Indecisive.* But sometimes they're useful."

"Agent Santos did not seem interested in some of my suggestions."

"Such as?"

"Reaching out to Russian immigrants who have an excellent communications network. I'm also looking into the word *hawqala,* to see if it has been used in the past. It seems like an unusual change of pace for someone delivering a message from a jihadist organization. Perhaps this will be a link we need to find and destroy a significant terror group."

We sat in silence for a few moments and then I said, "Do you have some personal beef with terrorists, or are you just focused on this asshole?"

"Russia has seen many more attacks than the US. Some are more public than others. It's a scourge that we would like to see neutralized. If it takes a little effort on our part to teach our friends in the United States how to best deal with extremist groups, then I am all for it."

"Let's hope we don't disappoint you."

She smiled and said, "Don't worry about it. Everyone disappoints me."

All I could say was, "Hard-line. I like it."

CHAPTER 12

LESS THAN AN hour after our first briefing, I found myself playing chauffeur to my Russian liaison, Darya Kuznetsova. She apparently had less use for bureaucracy than me. When Dan Santos said he had to go talk to his bosses and directed us to either sit tight or grab something to eat, Darya said, "I'm going to talk to some Russian speakers who might help us. Do you care to be part of such a conspiracy?"

Not only did she have the right idea, she worded the question perfectly. Next thing I knew, we were driving through Brooklyn on our way to Midwood. There were a lot of Russian immigrants from Midwood all the way to Brighton Beach, but I wasn't sure what information they could offer us.

As we were driving on the Ocean Parkway through Flatbush on our way to Midwood, Darya said, "These are ethnic Russians who lived in Kazakhstan. I don't want to explain why an NYPD detective is with me. Don't show your badge. I'll try to speak in English, but if we speak Russian, just smile and nod."

"Did you just tell me to be quiet and look pretty?" That got the laugh I intended.

"I hope that brain of yours is as sharp when we have to act quickly. I don't have a great deal of faith in your FBI."

"With an attitude like that you could be an *American* cop. We hate the FBI, too."

"I'm not a cop."

I didn't know exactly *what* Darya was, but I didn't get a chance to follow up, because we had arrived at our destination.

The first people we talked to were an elderly couple who lived on the first floor of a five-story walk-up. The man said virtually nothing but glared at me like I had stolen something from his bedroom. His giant, bald head reminded me of a pale watermelon.

The little knickknacks around the apartment could've been from any grandmother in the world. I liked a figurine of a burly man in a fur hat driving a wagon with an ox pulling it. It shouted "Russia."

The woman was better dressed than the man and evidently took care of herself. She agreed to speak English with Darya, and while she had a thick accent, I could still understand her.

Darya told me in a low voice as we walked through the apartment that the man still had ties to Kazakhstan and Russia. That was one of the reasons she didn't want to bring the FBI along with us. They just wouldn't understand.

She was also afraid the FBI would use heavy-handed tactics and threaten these people with everything from arrest to deportation—and ruin any chance of getting useful information.

The woman said, "Living in Kazakhstan can be hard in the

best of times. We went with a program to work as teachers at a school for Russian children. The climate is better than Moscow, but as we got older, it was still tough on our bodies. We had a chance to follow our oldest son here and have been quite happy for the past nine years."

Darya said, "Do you talk to others in the Kazakh community?"

"Of course. Every day."

I followed the conversation, but the woman's accent was sometimes tough to understand. I liked the way Darya showed her respect as if she were a daughter visiting a grandmother. The old man just stared on in silence.

Finally, Darya got to the meat of our questions. "Have you heard anyone talk about the attack yesterday?"

"Some. Mostly people just repeating things from the news."

I had considered this question and thought this would be a critical juncture in any interview. Do we reveal the fact that we think the driver was from Kazakhstan? It might make people pay attention.

Then Darya said, "We think the driver was a Kazakh."

The old woman was shocked. "How can this be? The Kazakhs have no real hatred for the United States. Is this some ploy to ship us all out? Do they want us all to move back to our homelands? We live here, but we've never trusted the government."

I said, "Neither do we. Governments try to trick people. But this isn't one of those times."

Then the old man mumbled something. I thought it was English.

I looked at him and said, "Did you say something, sir?"

The old man said it again and I heard it clearly: "Bullshit."

Apparently, he spoke the essential English words.

CHAPTER 13

AFTER WE TALKED to several other Russian families with ties to Kazakhstan, I decided to track down a couple of my informants as well.

Darya said, "I don't understand. If your informants are not Russian, what would they know about this?"

"These are the type of people that hear everything. Small things. Big things. We may get a tip about someone looking for a ride out of the city that could break open the case. The more ears we have listening the better chance we have to hear something."

"But none are Russian?"

"These people aren't Russian, but they're criminals, and criminals often trade in information."

Darya said, "If they're criminals why aren't they in jail?"

I had to shrug at that simple question. "Different reasons. Some are smart. Some are lucky. Some have good lawyers. You can't tell me all the criminals in Moscow are locked up."

"It depends on who is protecting them."

I laughed. "Here in America, we don't care who protects

who. We just found it's easier to let most criminals stay free. Keeps me in a job."

I could tell my Russian guest didn't agree with my flippant logic. I was curious to see how she reacted to some of my informants.

I added, "I also have some Russian mob people who occasionally help me. But these guys are easier to reach for now."

The first place I stopped was a gambling house in Flatbush. It was close and not too dangerous. A good test for Darya.

The small storefront on Foster Avenue looked like a simple diner. Busy, but simple. Few people realized that when you ordered one of only five things on the menu, you also got access to a variety of gambling opportunities from football to soccer in Asia.

I heard someone call out, "Hey, Mike." I smiled and waved at one of the gamblers I knew from somewhere. No one was alarmed to see me. They knew I was a homicide detective and this place was as safe as any in the city.

I ducked into a corridor past a heavy curtain. Darya followed right behind me. When we entered the rear room, a blond man with tattoos smearing his upper arms and neck jumped up in alarm until he recognized me.

He said, "Jesus, Mike, a little notice would be nice. You scared the crap out of me." Then he took a moment and didn't hide the fact that his eyes were wandering over Darya like she was a piece of meat for sale in the grocery store. He flashed a charming smile and said, "And who is this?"

Before I could say anything, Darya gave him a dazzling smile. Better than any I had earned. Maybe she was a softy for lowlife attention and cheap compliments.

My informant held out his hand and said, "Edward Lindell, at your service." Then he winked at her.

Darya grasped his hand and put her left hand over both of them like it was a warm greeting. Then she twisted quickly, put him in an arm bar, and drove Lindell's head into a table that held thousands of betting slips.

To make the point that she didn't care for the attention, Darya ran Lindell's head down the length of the table, using his face to push everything onto the floor.

Then she released her grip and watched him sprawl onto the dirty green linoleum floor that used to be part of the kitchen.

I suppressed a smile as I watched Ed Lindell get up on his hands and knees and shake his head to clear the stars.

"I think that was her way of saying she doesn't have time for your shit."

From the floor, Lindell said, "All she had to say was, 'Cut the shit.'"

"Frankly, I like her way better. But we're wasting time. We aren't here to watch you get the shit kicked out of you by a pretty woman. We need you to put out feelers about anything unusual related to someone trying to get out of the city or trying to buy a gun or explosives."

Lindell slowly rose to his feet and said, "This have to do with the bombing at the parade?"

"How did you know that?"

"Because I went to Penn State and I'm no idiot. That's all anyone is interested in right now. What will it get me?"

The universal question by informants. I thought about it and said, "Depends on what you give us. But it'll save you more lumps from this lady and you'll be in my good graces for a very, very long time."

Lindell said, "That and some toilet paper means I could take a shit."

Still without looking or acknowledging him, Darya raised a closed fist and caught Lindell across the left side of his face, knocking him against the wall and back onto the floor. She walked out without saying a word.

I nodded to Lindell on the floor and hustled out after Darya.

As we walked a block toward the car, she said, "You're not upset that I assaulted that man?"

"He's had worse. *I've* given him worse."

Darya said, "You don't want to know why I did it?"

"I assume you did it to hide the fact that you stole the 9 millimeter pistol he had sitting on the table." I didn't wait for an answer. I just held out my hand.

She slipped the gun out of her purse and laid it in my palm. "This is America. I'll be able to find a gun if I need it."

All signs pointed to her being a pretty good partner. I'd be able to work with her.

CHAPTER 14

THE NEXT MORNING everyone was in the task force meeting rooms early. Even some of the FBI agents seemed a little annoyed at all the planning and meetings we had gone through the day before. As far as I could tell, Darya and I were part of a handful that had actually gone out and done something. Not that we were telling anyone.

And of course, we started off the day with a stupid meeting. At least I thought it was stupid, until things got rolling.

Dan Santos went over some of the information they had learned the day before, including some of the forensic information from examining the destroyed truck.

Santos said, "There wasn't a lot to grab from the truck—mainly chemical residue that will be used to track down the exact manufacturer of the explosive. The ATF did manage to lift a fingerprint off the inside of the steering wheel, so we put a rush on it to every agency and database in the country. No hits came back. But our esteemed colleague from the Russian Embassy"—he turned and opened his hand toward Darya, as if he were a ringmaster announcing an act—"has found the print in a Russian military database."

Santos nodded to Darya, who stood up. She took a moment to gather her thoughts, as if she was trying to make the announcement more dramatic after the dull crime-scene analysis.

Darya said, "The fingerprint belongs to a thirty-one-year-old male named Temir Marat. His father was raised in Kazakhstan and his mother is an ethnic Russian. He spent his early years in Kazakhstan, then bounced back and forth between there and Russia."

I noticed everyone taking furious notes, but I still hadn't heard anything that would tell me where this asshole was.

Darya continued. "Marat served a stint in the Russian army, and that's how we got his fingerprint on file. He has no history of extremism, but the FBI says that's very common. There's little else known about him."

Someone from the back room called out, "Do we have a photograph of him?"

Darya shook her head. "It's printing now. It's five years old. It's from an application to the Moscow police. There is an older photo from when he entered the army, but he is much younger and he has a buzz cut."

I wrote one line in my little notebook. *Applied to police. Why?*

An Asian woman who worked for the FBI said, "I don't think a history of extremist views is necessary anymore. The way some of these groups recruit leads many without previous violent histories to join. In fact, it's a good move to recruit people not on any terrorist watch lists. This guy sounds like the perfect choice. Smart, unafraid of death, and able to blend in with the general population in the US. He could've been recruited from a website."

An Army major in uniform said, "I can see recruiting people inside the US like that, but this was someone living in Russia or Kazakhstan. There were some serious expenses. This is a step above some of the spur-of-the-moment attacks ISIS has inspired."

Dan Santos said, "It's hard to tell exactly what happened until we catch this guy. Our intelligence indicates that shifting to using trucks and cars and simple attacks like this has a major effect on public opinion. Anytime a group uses the fear of something common to exploit terror, they're eating away at our way of life. Berlin and Paris are perfect examples. There'll be kids there in ten years that jump at the sight of a truck. It's important that we move before this guy comes up with anything else to do."

Darya said, "Russia has seen some of this. Several attacks using trucks that plow into crowds."

When she sat down next to me I said, "I haven't seen those attacks in Russia on the news." This was a private conversation, not intended for the others.

"We don't have a need for everything to be public. Perhaps your government should try that approach occasionally."

I said, "Let's not get into a conversation about whose government is more effective."

"You're right, of course."

I said, "This wasn't some kid trying to get famous. I agree with our colleague in the Army. This attack was organized and funded. It was too big to try and keep quiet in a free country. The US government generally makes information about attacks public. Even if keeping things secret works for Russia, it's not the way we do things."

Darya smiled and said, "I know Americans have a fixation with fame and publicity. You also have many more TV networks than Russia. But sometimes it's better to handle things quietly and not cause a panic. I fear this is a lesson the US will have a chance to learn in the coming years."

I hoped that wasn't the case.

CHAPTER 15

DAN SANTOS SURPRISED me. As soon as our early morning briefing was done, he grabbed Darya and me and said, "I lined up some interviews we can do today."

I withheld any smartass comment, because I wanted to encourage this kind of behavior.

Darya looked bored, but stood up and gathered her things.

Santos said, "Pretty exciting, huh? Your first interviews on a major terror investigation."

I mumbled, "Yeah. Our first interviews. Exciting." I could barely meet Darya's eyes.

She had a wide grin, but Santos was too wrapped up in his own world to notice.

The first stop we made was in lower Manhattan near the NYU campus, a small deli on University Place. It was still early and the place was nearly empty.

I caught up to Dan, who was walking pretty fast from the car, and said, "Are you hungry? What would this deli have to offer us for the case?"

"It's not the deli, but who's working there." He pulled a photograph of a young man with a dark complexion and short-cropped, black hair. "His name is Abdul Adair, he's from the United Arab Emirates. He's studying biology at NYU and works here part-time."

"What led you to him?"

"What do you mean? He's a Muslim, first of all. He attends virtually all of the Muslim student union meetings, and we have intel that he has acted suspiciously and taken a lot of photographs of New York."

That response actually gave me more questions than answers, but I wanted to see how this would go. Santos had just described a college student who likes to sightsee.

We stepped in the doors and no one paid any attention to us, the sign of a good neighborhood. A couple of little kids chased the deli cat and a young mother lazily followed them while chatting on her cell phone. The smell of the chicken cutlet hero the cook was wrapping up for a customer reminded me I had forgotten to eat breakfast. My stomach growled.

Santos stepped to the counter and asked about Abdul. A minute later, we were sitting at a small table in the corner, next to a refrigerator stocked with smoothies that cost seven bucks each.

The student from the UAE was twenty-one and small. He couldn't have been over five foot five and 130 pounds, which made him look even younger. The kid was already trembling.

Santos spent a few minutes clarifying Abdul's information. The whole process only seemed to make the young man more nervous. I scooted my chair back slightly because I didn't want to be in the splash zone if he vomited.

Then Santos asked a series of questions. "Have you ever had contact with an organization that espouses jihad? Don't lie. I'll know if you're lying."

The young man vigorously shook his head.

"Do you or any of your friends know anyone involved in a group like that?"

This time Abdul thought about it, then shook his head. He said, "I spend most of my time either studying or working here."

Santos said, "What about the Muslim student union at NYU?"

"What about it? I go there to see my friends. Meet women."

"And what do you plan to use your degree in biology for?"

"This coming summer I have an internship at an institute in San Francisco doing cancer research. That might be what I'm interested in long-term." The young man seemed to be getting some confidence.

The FBI agent made notes, but didn't invite Darya or me to say anything at all.

Now Santos moved on to our case. He pulled up our photograph of Temir Marat and said, "Know him?"

Abdul shook his head.

"Where were you on Thanksgiving morning?"

"Having breakfast with the family of one of my professors who lives in the Village."

"We'll need his name and address. Now."

Santos pushed over a notebook for Abdul to write in. He made more notes and asked more questions, which Abdul answered quickly and clearly. Then the FBI man thanked him, but warned him not to leave the city. That was it. It felt more like a schoolyard bullying session than an interview. When Santos stood up and handed Abdul a card, I did the same thing. The only difference is, I smiled and winked at him when I gave him the card. He gave me a nervous smile and nod in return.

Then all three of us marched out of the deli.

Before we even got to the car, I had to say, "What the hell was that?"

"What was what?"

"Treating that kid like that! We have no reason to believe that he's done anything wrong. Why are we wasting time scaring kids to death?"

Santos stopped on the sidewalk and looked at me like I was a little kid who just asked a stupid question in class. "Do I have to remind you, Detective, that this is a *federal* case? It's not some cheap New York City misdemeanor or dead dope addict." Santos looked at Darya to see if she was interested in getting involved in the argument. Then he said, "The FBI has to look at the big picture and see if we can link different terror networks. It may not seem like it's helping much now, but it could pay off big later. Let me know when you solve a major terror case."

That stung a little bit. As I slipped into the Crown Victoria, I felt like I'd been told off pretty effectively.

CHAPTER 16

AFTER THE INTERVIEW with Abdul, I realized my time might be better utilized. I saw my opportunity when Santos was called to a boss's office to give an update on the investigation.

I tried to quietly slip out of the task force office, ready to tell anyone who asked that I was just going to lunch. It would take a while to drive out to Brighton Beach, the Brooklyn neighborhood with a high population of Russian immigrants. But I doubted anyone would miss me, especially Agent Dan Santos.

As I hustled down the corridor away from the office, I heard someone behind me. I turned to see Darya Kuznetsova with a smile on her face.

She said, "Going somewhere?"

"Yeah, I'm going to do my job." Then, for no real reason, I said, "I'm going to visit some Russian mobsters. Do you want to come?"

She didn't say a word but just kept following me.

"Why didn't we talk to these Russians yesterday when we talked to your other informants?"

"Because Russian mobsters are in a different class. They

could help us, or they could try to find Marat themselves for a reward."

Darya said, "Do you think every Russian living in the US is a mobster?"

"That's ridiculous. Not everyone can be a mobster. Some Russians work in support roles." I waited until she turned and stared at me, then laughed and said, "I'm just kidding. But if you think no Russians are involved in organized crime, you're just as wrong. I know a couple of them. I know they won't be happy about the attack. So why don't we use that?"

That seemed to satisfy Darya and she stayed quiet, but alert, all the way through Brighton Beach. I pulled off Neptune Avenue a few blocks from our destination.

I parked away from the apartment we were headed to. No sense in alerting everyone by driving an NYPD Impala, whether it was marked or not, into one of the tightest, most isolated communities in New York.

Darya said, "What are you hoping to find out?"

"I just want to see if anyone knows anything about Marat. These guys won't have any loyalty to a terrorist. Terror attacks hurt their bottom line. They'll listen for information if we tell them what to listen for."

We walked up to the second-floor apartment, which offered a glimpse of the Atlantic if you angled your gaze just right.

I told Darya, "This guy we're going to see goes by different names. I'll wait until we see him to tell you what his name is now."

A wiry man with a disturbingly dark tan and a cigarette dangling from his mouth answered the door and just stared at us for a moment. He was about forty but looked older. He said, "What a surprise. I have no idea why you are visiting me now. I've been a very good boy lately." He ushered us inside. It was a surprisingly comfortable apartment, even if it did stink of cigarette smoke and beer. He plopped down in an oversize recliner while Darya and I eased onto a leather couch.

I said, "It's nice to see you too, Mr...."

"Vineyard. Lewis Vineyard. Good name, eh?"

"Yeah, I guess."

The Russian said in accented English, "I like it. I figure I work on my English, no one will ever suspect who or what I am."

I shrugged and said, "Except for the fact that you live in Brighton Beach, work at a Russian mob-run bar, and sell drugs and guns to Russian mobsters, I doubt anyone would ever suspect you of being a Russian criminal. I'm sure everyone will assume you're Swiss."

He gave me a smile and said, "That's my hope." Then he turned his attention to Darya. "And who's this lovely creature you brought to my home? If you're looking for a place for her to live, I agree. She can even have my bedroom."

Darya didn't say a word and I immediately realized she didn't want this guy knowing she was Russian as well. It was also useful for people to not realize she spoke their language.

He held up his arms to show off his tan and said, "You'd love it, baby. I sit on the beach every single day. You would, too, if you were raised in a place like Moscow." He gazed into her face and said, "With soft, white skin like that, you could be a Russian beauty yourself."

I said, "This is my colleague. And we're here about something serious."

"I'm listening." Then he threw in, "And what's in it for me?"

"We're working with the feds on this, so there could be some decent reward money."

He clapped his rough hands together and rubbed them. "Sounds good to me." He stubbed out the cigarette in an overflowing ashtray.

I said, "It's about the attack on the parade Thursday. I'm looking for any information about a Russian-speaking suspect. If there's anyone unusual in the area. If there've been strange requests for guns or explosives. Anything you can think of."

Lewis Vineyard said, "I deal mostly with people I know already. But I'll keep my ears open. No one wants to see shit like that happen. There were little kids killed."

"And we're going to catch that son of a bitch."

CHAPTER 17

WE STOPPED AT a few other places in Brighton Beach, but none seemed as promising as Lewis Vineyard. He knew everyone and dealt with everyone. I was confident he'd come up with something.

Darya said, "I can see why these people leave Russia. They left food lines, and found decent weather and good housing. It's hard to compete with America head-to-head. Even your marketing is better than ours."

"What do you mean?"

"You have *land of the free* or *the streets paved with gold*. We have *plenty of land to farm if you don't mind freezing in Siberia*."

I laughed at that.

She gave me a smile and said, "It would be interesting to work with you on a daily basis."

"Let's catch this guy first, then see where it goes."

"And when we catch him, what happens to him next?"

"The FBI will bleed him for information. On everything."

"That's what we thought."

Before I could ask her what that meant—that "we"—my

phone rang. I looked down and saw it was my grandfather. I never like to ignore calls from Seamus because it could be something serious, the fear always associated with an elderly relative's calls.

"Seamus, everything all right?"

His chuckle told me he was fine. "It's not like I'm going to keel over at any minute. I may still be in my prime. It's a new millennium. Age is just a number."

"The fact that you've seen the last few millennia makes me worry about your health."

"For a change, I'm calling to help you with your job."

"How are you going to do that?"

"As a man of the cloth, I have friends in every denomination. One of them happens to be a Muslim cleric. He's the imam of a mosque in Queens."

"I appreciate that, Seamus, but we're not really taking the shotgun approach that all Muslims know about terror attacks."

"But this imam spent some time in Kazakhstan. If I overheard you correctly on the phone last night, Kazakhstan has something to do with your investigation."

All I could say was, "Give me the info."

Twenty minutes later, we were in Jamaica Estates, pulling up to a mosque off the Grand Central Parkway near 188th Street.

As soon as we were out of the car, a small man who looked about sixty-five approached us. He was wearing a suit with a collarless white shirt and a small, white cap.

The man gave us a warm smile as he said, "You can't be

Seamus's grandson, Michael, can you? I am Adama Nasir."
He had a slight accent that was hard to place. His wire-
rimmed glasses gave him the look of a scholar.

I took his hand and said, "I am Seamus's grandson. He's
much older than he pretends to be." I introduced Darya as my
associate.

We stayed outside and strolled through a playground for the
school attached to the mosque. Nasir explained that he was
born in Qatar and had traveled throughout the world as a visiting scholar of the Koran. I noted that he had spent two years in
Kazakhstan.

Nasir said, "Your grandfather mentioned what you were doing. I think it's important for Muslims to spread the truth that,
just like Christians, the vast majority of Muslims just want to
worship in peace. Most Muslims are outraged at attacks like the
one on the parade."

I said, "I can appreciate the sentiment, but right now I'm
only interested in catching who's responsible. It doesn't matter
to me what religion he is or even what his motivation was. We
need to catch him before he does anything else."

"That's why I asked your grandfather if I could speak with
you, because he mentioned that there was a possibility the suspect was from Kazakhstan. There is a bar in Rockaway Park
that's a meeting place for ethnic Russians with connections to
Kazakhstan. It's really quite a festive place. I have visited it myself because of my stay in Kazakhstan. Of course, I couldn't
drink alcohol, but the company was invigorating. If anyone

knows about someone from Kazakhstan looking to hide in the greater New York area, it's that crowd."

This was a good lead. Probably more than the FBI had. I thanked him and turned with Darya to head for our car.

Nasir said, "I hope you find who you're looking for. It's a tricky business, these attacks. I've seen it all over the Middle East. Some are based on religious conviction. Some people are forced to do the attacks and some attacks are not what they seem."

I said, "Not what they seem in what way?"

"I used to see it in occupied Palestine. They've been known to kill other Palestinians in attacks so that Israel is blamed. I've even heard rumors that some of the old Israeli governments allowed attacks in Jerusalem so that they would have a reason to respond. There is a certain return on this philosophy."

He was right, but I didn't see the US government allowing an attack like this. I also couldn't see them putting so many resources into catching someone if they had allowed the attack to occur.

All we could do was follow up on the leads we had.

CHAPTER 18

THE STREETS FELT more alive than ever on the drive to Rockaway Park. It was incredible. Even with the cold weather, people were out in the streets, as if telling the terrorists, "New Yorkers don't hide."

The bar was on Rockaway Beach Boulevard, not far from the Jacob Riis Park. As soon as we stepped in the door, I heard conversation in Russian.

Darya was right behind me as I surveyed the long room with booths on the left and stools against the bar on the right. Bright sunlight crashed through the wide bay windows, saving the place from the usual depressing air of a bar in the middle of the day.

It was also surprisingly crowded, with people shouting good-naturedly from one booth to another while the bartenders called out orders in Russian.

I wasn't sure what to do, so without identifying myself, I told the bartender I was looking for someone. I showed him the picture of Marat and told him he was a Russian, speaking Kazakh.

The burly bartender scratched his red beard and shook his

head and said in English, "No, no, I never seen this man. Sorry. What you want to drink?"

I bought two beers and settled in at the bar with Darya. There were several other women in the place, but the way they were sitting in booths by themselves or with one man led me to believe they might be prostitutes. I hoped no one would make a mistake and approach Darya. For their sake.

I watched our bartender speaking in a low voice in Russian to one of his colleagues, not far from us.

Darya leaned in close and said, "The bartender just said the two men at the end of the bar are looking for the same man we are."

Having Darya undercover was brilliant. They didn't seem to care if we overheard them speaking Russian.

I looked over to the far end of the bar where there were two men standing, dressed in cheap suits with ties, about my age, but heavy and out of shape. One of the men was burly, with a pockmarked face, and the other had cold, gray eyes, and as soon as they met mine I realized someone at the bar had just told them who I was asking about.

I assumed he made me for a cop, because he made no move to come over to talk. That was fine by me. His interest didn't concern me.

I formulated a plan, and appreciated the fact that Darya didn't ask what it was.

After a few minutes, the two men in suits stepped out the back door of the bar and into the narrow parking lot. We wasted no time going out the main door and into the same lot.

I saw them get into a new Lincoln. Comfortable, but not flashy. Once we got into my Impala, I ran the tag quickly and it came back to a moving company owned by Russians. Shocking.

When it didn't look like they were going anywhere, I said to Darya, "Sometimes we have to make our own karma."

All she said was, "I agree."

As we slipped out of the car, I said, "Whatever happens in Rockaway Park stays in Rockaway Park. Is that a problem?"

"Not unless you expect me to dig a hole if you kill them. I hate to dig."

"I'll keep that in mind."

Both the men were still sitting in the car, looking out at the traffic trickling by on Rockaway Beach Boulevard.

I was careful, trying to approach the car from behind and in the blind spot. As we got closer, I realized they were taking a smoke break with both the windows open.

Neither seemed to be monitoring the mirrors. For a couple of mobsters, they weren't terribly observant.

They couldn't have set it up better for me.

CHAPTER 19

I LIKED HOW both men stayed calm and didn't jump when I appeared in the driver's-side window. I crouched low so my face filled the window, and rested my arms across the door with my Glock service weapon in my right hand, casually hanging into the car.

I said, "Hello, fellas, how's your day going?"

The driver, the burly man with a pockmarked face, mumbled, "No English. Go 'way."

"You think you're the first one to pull that kind of shit on me? There is a universal cure for those who don't want to speak English." Without hesitation, I pulled the door handle, reached into the Lincoln, and grabbed the man with two fingers behind his jaw. The pressure made him hop out of the car with no help from me other than the two fingers on his sensitive nerves that ran there.

I spun him around and slammed him into the car.

I was prepared to order the other man out, but he jumped out on his own to help his friend. Just as he reached the rear of the Lincoln, Darya sprang out from behind the car parked next to them. I had no idea what she did, but the guy was on the asphalt in a heartbeat.

I said to her, "You okay?"

She said, "Good."

She was careful to keep her words to a minimum, because even though her accent is barely discernible, she didn't want these Russians to pick up that she knew their language.

I focused on the man I had in an arm bar against the car. I patted him down quickly and pulled out a Ruger 9mm from his waistband. Holding him with one hand, I holstered my Glock and stuck his Ruger in my pants.

I said, "If you don't speak English, you're under arrest for carrying a concealed weapon. If you do speak English, I'll talk to you for a minute."

He said in a remarkably clear voice, "We speak English."

"Good. See how easy that was?" I eased up slightly on my arm bar, then stepped back and let the man face me. I said, "Now, why were you asking about Temir Marat?"

"Who?"

I grabbed his arm again to show him I could get rough if I had to. That's when he surprised me. He was fast for a big guy. He twisted his body and then landed a knee right on my thigh. It hurt. I mean, in an it-made-me-want-to-pee kind of hurt.

I staggered back and he immediately threw two punches at my head. He had some style and looked like he'd boxed at some point in his life. That's probably how he landed a job like this.

I had done a little boxing myself and immediately had my

guard up, fending off his punches. As I stepped back, I saw that Darya, still alert and on top of her man, was watching what was happening.

I let the guy in front of me take a wild swing. I ducked the right fist as it just grazed the top of my head. Then I twisted hard and landed a left, low on his back, right in his kidneys. Ouch—I knew from experience that that location was *painful*.

I spun to his other side and kneed him in the left thigh, making sure things were equal. Then I grabbed him by the groin with my left hand and by the throat with my right hand, and bull-rushed him backward into a parked pickup truck.

He let out an *umphf* as the air rushed out of him. Then I put him on the ground close to his partner.

The partner tried to sit up and Darya blasted him with a forearm right across the back of his head. I could hear his nose crush against the asphalt; blood started to leak out and pool into puddles near his face.

I said to the guy I had on the ground, "This is serious shit. For all I know, you were involved in the attack on the parade. That's why you're about to have the worst day of your life."

The man sputtered, "Wait, wait. It's not what you think."

"Then tell me what it is."

"I don't want to get in more trouble."

"You can't get in more trouble. You're carrying a gun illegally and you assaulted a police officer."

"I don't want to get in more trouble by talking."

I sat there for a moment and thought about it. Darya looked

up at me expectantly. Finally, I said, "Tell me what you want to tell me. Anything you say while I have you on the ground like this is free. Total immunity."

"If I tell you the truth, you let us go?"

"That depends on how much of the truth you tell me."

The man thought about it for a moment, then said, "I don't know your man, Marat. I have the same photo you showed the bartender. Someone contracted us to take him out."

"A mob hit on a terrorist? Why?"

"*Why* is not one of the questions we ask in my line of business."

"Where did you get the photo of him?"

"It was in an envelope with some cash and instructions to find him and kill him." After another moment he said, "That's the truth, the whole truth."

I released my grip and let him sit up. He brushed off a couple of pebbles that were lodged in his face. One of them perfectly filled the biggest pockmark on his left cheek.

I looked at him and said, "Surprisingly, I do believe you."

I got a little more information out of the other, but stuck to my promise to release them. Besides, I had gotten the information through an illegal interrogation. There was nothing I could do to them.

After I stood up, I took his Ruger out of my waistband, took it apart, and tossed two pieces in a sewer drain. He started to object, then kept his mouth shut. I would toss the rest of the pistol, including the magazine, down a few different drains on our way back to Manhattan. I appreciated his groan as the gun disappeared.

I stepped over to the other man standing next to Darya and started to pat him down. Just as I did, the man said, "She took it already."

I gave Darya a look and she reached in her purse, then pulled out a Smith & Wesson revolver. She shrugged as she slipped it into the palm of my hand.

She gave me a smile and said, "A girl has got to try."

CHAPTER 20

AFTER WE TALKED to the Russian mobsters, I drove us back to the task force headquarters. Darya said she had calls to make based on some of the information we'd found. We agreed to meet up later.

She was very quiet on the ride back, and I found myself wondering what her role in all this was. Dan Santos trusted her, and even though he was a fed I didn't think he'd put someone in the middle of the investigation who couldn't be trusted. But still, something nagged at me. The moment I got to my desk, my cell rang. I didn't recognize the caller, a man's voice with a thick Russian accent. He said his name and I still couldn't place it. Then I realized who it was: the silent husband of the woman we had spoken to in Midwood yesterday. The only English word he had said was, "Bullshit."

Now he spoke in halting English. I guess Darya's idea of not letting people know you spoke their language wasn't a unique trick.

I said, "What can I do for you?"

"When you and the pretty Russian woman came here—we told truth."

He spoke slowly and carefully so I could understand him. Aside from the accent, his English was not bad at all.

I said, "But some of your truth has changed since we were there?" I was trying to think how he had reached me, then I remembered that Darya had written my number as well as her own on a sheet of paper.

"Nothing has changed, except I met someone who might know the man you're looking for. He gave me some information that I thought you might use."

On every big case, there are thousands of leads. God help me, but I was a sucker for someone giving me new information, even if the odds of it being accurate or useful were small.

The old man said, "A man I ran into said he knows the family of the man who did this terrible crime."

"In Russia or Kazakhstan?"

"In New Jersey."

That caught me by surprise and made me pull a notepad from the FBI desk I was sitting at. I couldn't help but look around the room to make sure no one was eavesdropping on my conversation. Technically, all official leads were supposed to be put into a computer program for review before anyone followed up on them.

I said, "It's interesting he has family in New Jersey. That's nothing I had heard."

The old man said, "There are lots of Russians trying to live the right way. Many of us fled terrible conditions and appreciate all the advantages we have here in United States. Most Russians are perfectly respectable. It might not seem like it in your line of work, where everyone is a potential suspect. But this isn't Russia. You can't think that way."

"I don't generally think that way about any group. Nevertheless, I am a cop and I have to follow up on leads. Can you narrow down where his family might live in New Jersey?"

"A little community called Weequahic, in Newark. The name you're looking for is Konstantin Nislev."

"Do you want to give me some details about the person who gave you this information?"

"No. No, I don't." Then the phone went dead.

If nothing else, it gave me another excuse to get out of the Federal Building for a few hours. With Manhattan's usual Saturday traffic, I knew I could be in the car for a while.

A little work in Google and in the New Jersey public records database gave me an address for a Konstantin Nislev, right where the old man said he'd be.

Traffic wasn't as bad as I feared, and I was cruising past neat row houses in the Newark community of Weequahic. I found a parking spot just across from where I was going. I sat there for a minute, checking out the situation.

It was a well-kept row house, and an old oak tree rose up from the front yard and sent branches toward the house like a giant monster. Other than that, the yard was immaculate. Just a few short strips of grass and a lot of decorative stones. It looked like a comfortable home.

I stepped out of the car and tried to look casual as I walked up toward the front door. But I didn't feel casual. If this lead was accurate, it was a big deal. A *giant* deal. So big I might have a hard time explaining to the FBI how I managed to get the lead, not file it in the proper system, not tell anyone where I was going, and then question the suspect's family.

It was probably nothing.

I rang the bell and heard soft chimes on the inside of the house. A moment later, a man who looked about sixty, with thinning hair, wearing heavy-framed glasses, answered the front door.

He smiled and had a noticeable accent when he said, "May I help you?"

I held up my badge and said, "Konstantin Nislev?"

The man said, "I wondered how long it would take the authorities to find us."

CHAPTER 21

I SAT ON a couch with an uncomfortable wooden frame on the back. I took the tea that Konstantin's wife, Vera, offered as we all chatted in a small living room almost overwhelmed with photographs.

Temir Marat's aunt and uncle had heard through the Russian grapevine that he was a suspect in the attack on Thanksgiving. The older couple didn't deny the relation, or that they were worried about their nephew.

I gave them a few minutes to settle down and we chatted about other things before I got to the serious questions on my mind.

I said, "You have a lot of photos of Seton Hall."

Konstantin said, "I have been the facilities manager there for five years. I was an engineer in Russia, and it fit in perfectly with the needs of the university when I started to look for a job here."

"How long have you been in the US?"

"We moved here about six years ago. I had lived in the US before for extended periods, while I worked on different projects for a construction company based in Switzerland. My children and the rest of the family came over four years ago."

"And your nephew, Temir?"

Vera answered that one. "We were hoping he would come with his cousins four years ago, but he had a wife who was pregnant, and already had one young child at home."

"Where was he living?"

"Moscow." I just nodded and let the story continue.

"Temir had a decent job doing something for either the city or the Russian government. He had a nice apartment and a little bit of money. He speaks English so I thought he might want to come. But he decided to stay."

"When's the last time you talked to him?"

"He always sends me mail on special occasions," Vera said. "He loves his aunt Verochka."

"And you had no idea he was here in the US?"

"None at all."

"Do you have any photographs of your nephew?"

Vera stood up quickly and went to a series of framed photographs sitting on a bookshelf. She walked back with a particularly large one that showed a group of more than twenty-five people.

Vera pointed to a young man, no more than fourteen or fifteen, in the corner of the photo. "That is Temir. This was at a family gathering in Moscow about fifteen years ago. His father had died and we thought it was important for him to have male role models. Konstantin's brothers all spent time with him."

"Do you have any idea when he might've become radicalized and interested in attacking the US?"

Konstantin said, "I'm not sure I understand. Radicalized in what way?"

"Had his belief in Islam twisted to where he felt he needed to participate in a jihad?"

Konstantin said, "That's ridiculous. I don't understand any of that. We're not Muslim. We are Russian Orthodox. The whole family is Russian Orthodox. We are all, to my knowledge, devout and law abiding. Are you sure you have the right suspect?"

Suddenly I had some doubts. They had identified their nephew through the photograph I had. The ATF had taken the fingerprint from the truck used in the bombing. I had fought the man in the photograph hand-to-hand. He was the right suspect, but did we have the correct motive?

I'd have a lot of explaining to do when I got back to Manhattan.

CHAPTER 22

AFTER I'D INTERVIEWED Temir Marat's family in New Jersey, I took my time driving back to the Federal Building. I lingered in the lobby and called home to make sure everything was all right. Then, God help me, I sneaked back into the task force office. I felt sheepish, like a dog who had peed on the carpet.

Now I had to figure out how to explain my trip to New Jersey and all the interesting information I'd found out.

Darya was working on some notes at a table on the side. When I sat down next to her, I noticed the report was written in Cyrillic.

Darya glanced up and said, "When I'm in Moscow, I write in English. It's quite convenient. Like my own secret code. Because no one tries to learn anyone else's languages anymore."

I said, "Thanks, grandma, for the lecture. Besides, you've been with me during most of the investigation. There's nothing you could write that I haven't already heard firsthand. Probably from someone with a thick Russian accent."

"Where have you been?"

"Jersey."

Darya gave me a smile and said, "Seeing a girlfriend?"

"Ha, that's funny. Until I think about my Irish fiancée. Then it's scary. If I went to see a girlfriend in New Jersey, it would probably be my last trip to New Jersey ever."

Darya said, "While you have been out sightseeing, your friend the FBI agent and I have come up with an interesting wrinkle."

"What's that?"

"We've found the phrase Marat said before detonating the bomb, *hawqala,* the one that means 'There is no power nor strength save by Allah.'"

I said, "What do you mean you 'found' it?"

Just then Dan Santos strutted up to us and said, "It's a phrase that has been used by people being blackmailed into committing an attack." He looked between Darya and me, then just kept talking. "A Georgian soldier said it before he detonated an explosive vest at a police station, killing eleven, including himself. Turns out his mother was being held by a group that forced him into the attack. Apparently Georgians love their mothers."

"What happened to his mother?"

Darya answered. "They released her. They want people to believe them when they say they'll release someone for carrying out an attack."

Then Santos said, "Last year a former Russian security agent said *hawqala* before he charged a speaker at a meeting of businessmen in Chechnya. He managed to kill the mayor and a deputy with a hand grenade. The mayor was opposed to Russian influence in Chechnya. That attacker survived four bullets by security. He said he'd been told to do it. He regretted it. He also said the reason he shouted *hawqala* was because he heard it would show he wasn't a monster. It's a weird situation. The military and some law enforcement types know the phrase. This is the first time it's been used outside the former Soviet Union. It might be the wave of the future."

That all started to make sense with what I had just learned in New Jersey. Now I had to find a way to tell them I'd been working on my own.

I looked at Darya and realized I wasn't built for keeping secrets. I just started to talk. "I've developed some information I want to discuss with the two of you."

Neither of them offered any encouragement so I kept going.

"I got a tip that Temir Marat had family that lived in Newark."

Darya said, "Right here in the US."

I nodded.

Santos said, "Did you put the lead into the system?"

"Not yet." I paused, but I could have been just as easily yelling, *I ignored you and went out on my own*. Instead, I said, "I wanted to make sure it wasn't a prank."

Santos calmly said, "I'm listening."

"So to ensure the information was good, I took a ride across the river."

Santos glared at me and raised his voice. "What?"

It was about as emotional as I had seen an FBI agent.

Santos said, "Was there something not clear about your place in this task force and how the investigation was going to be conducted?"

I shook my head. "All I can say is that it was not a prank. Marat's aunt and uncle moved here years ago and are still in touch with their nephew."

Now Santos slipped into the chair next to me and said, "Tell me everything they said."

"Oh, so I can't break the rules unless I find out something important?"

"No, but this case is bigger than politics."

I ran down the information I had gathered from Konstantin and Vera Nislev.

Both Darya and Santos took notes with interest.

Finally, when I had come clean and told them everything, Dan Santos looked at me and said, "This is good stuff. Now collect your shit and hit the road."

I stared at him for a moment. "What are you talking about?"

"It's a privilege to work on a case like this, on a task force like this. We all have certain procedures and everyone was briefed. Yet you are the only one who decided to go out on his own."

Darya started to come to my defense and I was afraid she was going to mention our earlier interviews. I held up a hand to stop her. I knew when a decision had been made. It didn't matter why it was made.

Without saying a word or acting like a spoiled brat, I picked up my notebook and a few other things I needed and strolled out of the task force with my head held high.

CHAPTER 23

THAT EVENING, I sat on the couch after dinner and doodled on a pad, making a few notes and my own version of a chart that showed the connection between everyone in the case.

The only call to the NYPD I had made since I left the FBI was to my lieutenant, Harry Grissom. I told him exactly what had happened, what I had found out, and that I had been told to leave. His response was pure Harry.

Grissom said, "On the bright side, at least you weren't kicked off the task force for stealing something."

I gave him half a chuckle.

He said, "Seriously, Mike, this isn't going to change anything between us or on the squad. Maybe some bosses will be pissed off, but they're so used to the FBI bullshit that I doubt anyone will care. I'll talk to Santos, then call you back when things have leveled out."

That made me feel better. Seeing the kids and having one last dinner of Thanksgiving leftovers set my head on straight. I also decided that just because I wasn't officially on the task force investigating the attack on the parade, that didn't mean I couldn't do anything about it. I was still a cop.

Now I was a pissed-off cop. And I wanted to find out what the hell was going on. Things were not as they appeared, and my unrelenting need to understand events kept pushing me.

Jane plopped down on the couch next to me and said, "What'cha workin' on?"

"Nothing, really. Just putting a few thoughts down on paper."

She laid her head on my shoulder and pointed at the page where I'd been doodling and said, "I especially like your thoughts about this boat and the giant shark behind it. Did you watch *Jaws* again last night?"

I let out a laugh. "No, but I'll let you in on a little secret."

She turned that beautiful face toward me and looked at me like I was about to explain the meaning of life.

I said, "The only things I can draw are boats, sharks, and swords. Anything else looks like a chimpanzee grabbed the pencil."

Jane said, "That's incredible. I'm in the same boat."

"You can only draw a few things?"

"No. Mine is with reading. I can really zip through novels I like by great writers like Michael Connelly and Tess Gerritsen. But when I read the history books I'm assigned at school, I just can't get into them. Now that I know it's just a family issue, I won't worry about it as much."

Even though I liked her sly smile, I said, "Sorry, that's not gonna cut it. It's an interesting argument and I admire the effort that went into it, but you'll read every history book assigned or I'll try to draw your portrait and post it at school."

Jane said, "I like that kind of out-of-the-box thinking. You're turning out to be a pretty good parent."

That was the kind of praise I needed about now.

I was still smiling at the remark a few minutes later when my phone rang and I heard Harry Grissom's voice. As usual, he got right to the point.

"Mike, it was too hard to listen to that jerk-off Santos. He was jabbering on about you not following regulations. But all I could say was, 'So what else is new?'"

A smile crept across my face, though I'd been dreading this call.

Grissom said, "I've never seen them quite like this before."

I said half-jokingly, "So you don't want me to show up at the FBI office tomorrow?"

"I don't even want you to show up at an NYPD office tomorrow. You've earned a day or two off. Enjoy yourself."

If I was a good parent, Harry Grissom was a great lieutenant.

CHAPTER 24

I SPENT SUNDAY with the family and on Monday was up early to make sure everyone got off to school without a hitch. It was fun. We played a couple of quick games over breakfast and on the short ride to Holy Name. We even arrived more than five minutes early. I was afraid it might give Sister Sheila a heart attack.

She surprised me with a simple smile and wave.

I ran some errands, cleaned up the apartment, and in general sulked about not being at the task force. Then, in the afternoon, I stopped in to say hello to my grandfather. He was busy at his desk when I walked through the front door of the administrative offices for the church.

I said, "What are you working on, old man?" I expected a smart-aleck reply.

Instead, Seamus said, "I've got to get this grant into the city before the close of business today."

"Since when do you worry about grants?"

"Since I want a way to bring kids in the neighborhood, who aren't Catholic and don't attend the school, to an afterschool program that would include a meal and tutoring."

"That sounds like a worthy project."

"At my age I only work on worthy projects." He set down his pen and looked up at me. "Is this how you're going to spend a precious day off? Harassing an elderly clergyman? Do you think you could find something better to do with your time?"

A broad smile spread across my face. "It's odd to have the shoe on the other foot for a change. You know how usually I'm trying to work and you're bugging me about something. How does it feel?"

Seamus said, "You tell me. How does it feel to block my efforts to bring underprivileged kids in for a snack and extra tutoring every day?"

"Okay, you win this round, old man. But I'll be back." Just then, my phone rang. I said to Seamus, "You were saved by the bell."

I backed out of the office as I answered the phone. I didn't recognize the number. "This is Michael Bennett." I shaded my eyes from the afternoon sun.

"And this is Lewis Vineyard."

It took me a second to realize that was my Russian mob informant's new name. At least one he was trying out. "I'm a little surprised to hear from you."

Lewis said, "We need to meet. Today."

I thought about explaining that I was off duty, but I could tell by the tone of his voice he needed to see me. We picked a diner we both knew on the West Side.

I said, "What do you got? Did you find Temir Marat?"

"No. But I know where he'll be tonight."

CHAPTER 25

LEWIS VINEYARD HAD hooked me. I wanted to meet with him right away, but he said he couldn't. He had other commitments. And it would look suspicious if he slipped away right now. He met me four hours later, at a diner near West End Avenue. I knew that meant he was serious. He didn't want to risk any of his Russian friends in Brooklyn seeing us together. I was in the booth waiting for him thirty minutes early. I never did that. It took me a moment to notice Lewis coming down the street toward the front door. I craned my neck to look out the window at my overly tan informant wearing a nice button-down shirt and jeans. He almost looked respectable. He was dark, but not leathery; he hadn't started spending all his time in the sun until the last few years.

As soon as he plopped into the booth across from me I said, "It's not cool to tease me with important information, then not meet me immediately."

He held up his hands to calm me down and said, "No way around it. I called you as soon as I had the information, but things got hopping around the bar and I couldn't just leave. And there was no way I could have you show up there."

"I believe that the information you have is good, otherwise you wouldn't come all the way up here to see me."

Lewis said, "It's nice to see how the other half lives. Just walking down the street, I'd say you guys live pretty good up here. I prefer Brighton Beach. But that's just me."

I couldn't wait any longer. "If you're done with your monologues about New York City, can you tell me where Marat will be tonight?"

"It's not quite that easy. This is worth a lot."

I said, "What about the time there was a hit on you and I stopped the hitter in Brooklyn Heights? What was that worth?" I just stared at him and waited for an answer.

"You have a point. You've never screwed me, and you help me out. So I'm going to give you this information—if you tell me you'll make the FBI pay. This is so big the NYPD won't have the cash."

"I doubt that."

His smile told me he had some good info. Finally, I nodded and said, "If it's good information, I'll do everything I can to get you paid. That's the best I can promise."

Lewis Vineyard said, "That's good enough for me." Now he took a moment to gather his thoughts and glanced around the diner to make sure no one was close enough to hear us speak.

Lewis said, "Your man, Marat, will be at the Harbor House, down by Battery Park, at eight p.m. tonight. He may be meeting someone there. A couple members of the Russian mob are going to intercept him."

"How do you know that information so precisely?"

Lewis perked up and said, "I sold them the guns. Two SIG P220s. It's a shame they'll probably toss them in the river after the hit. They're some nice guns just to use one time."

I looked down at my watch and realized I didn't have much time. I didn't have time to verify the information or even scope out the restaurant. But that's how things with informants usually worked.

CHAPTER 26

I RACED SOUTH on West End Avenue until I could slip onto the Joe DiMaggio Highway. It was too late to call in the troops and plan anything worthwhile. Besides, this could still all be bullshit. I'd know soon enough.

I had to catch myself when I realized I was driving like a lunatic. My driving was the reason people always cursed at New Yorkers. I cut off a UPS truck and tried to wave my apology to a heavyset driver who was not happy.

I'd zipped past all the Trump buildings, some with plywood hiding his name. The vents for the Lincoln and Holland tunnels barely registered on my right.

I tried calling Darya, just so someone knew what was happening. No answer. I didn't leave a message.

Now I started to consider the questions that were popping into my head. Why would someone pay the mob to kill a terrorist? Who gained from his death? Were the local Russians worried about backlash? Did they really love America that much, or was it their bottom line? All the same questions any homicide detective would ask.

I didn't know the answer to any of them.

I didn't call Harry Grissom. There was no need to put him in the trick bag if I screwed this up. I had to let things unfold.

And I wanted Temir Marat alive. I had questions to ask him before he was in FBI custody and no one got to talk to him again.

It was true, our last meeting had not gone the way I planned. He was tough and he had skills like no one I had seen in a long time. But I was determined. I had my Glock. And I had a backup revolver on my ankle.

I was as ready as I would ever be.

I exited the highway just before the tunnel that would loop me around to the East Side, parking illegally before I started running through the maze of parks and benches before the water. I scouted the area thoroughly, hoping to see Marat out in public. What the hell, it seemed to happen all the time—fugitives caught by someone who was keeping their eyes open. There had been a baseball hat in my car, left there after the last police league softball game of the season. I'd pulled it on as low as I could, since Marat would no doubt recognize me.

I didn't see him, so as I approached the Pier A Harbor House, I slowed down to take it all in, peering into some of the windows that didn't face the water. I finally stepped inside.

The heat inside the restaurant made me realize how strong the chill in the air was, which I hadn't registered as I ran there. I scouted for other exits and windows while standing in the corner of the bar, noting that a long bar led to the dining room.

There was no one here I recognized. Lewis Vineyard had told me that one of the hitters who bought the guns from him was a well-built man about my height in his early forties, with a distinguishing characteristic of a purple birthmark on his cheek below his left eye. Lewis said the man worked with a tall female who had long black hair. There was no one that fit either of those descriptions that I could see.

I stepped farther into the restaurant, then saw someone I recognized. And frankly, it caught me by surprise. I might even say it shocked me. Sitting alone at a table by a window overlooking the river was Darya Kuznetsova.

What the hell?

I was about to get her attention when it hit me. This couldn't be a coincidence. What was she doing here? Was she luring Marat to be killed by the Russian mob? Why? Why not do it with her own government people?

That line of questioning led me to wonder—why had she provided a photo of Marat if she just intended to kill him?

Then I understood. At least that part of it. She didn't have a clue where Marat was hiding. The more people looking for him, the better.

She's the one who spread the word in the Russian community. That's how his aunt and uncle knew he was a suspect, why Konstantin said, "I wondered how long it would take the authorities to find us."

Shit. I was a fool.

CHAPTER 27

ONCE I MADE up my mind, I didn't dawdle. I stepped up, crossed the room, and sat down directly across from Darya Kuznetsova. I removed my hat like a gentleman, and smiled as if I were her date.

The look on her face and the way her eyes darted around the room told me she didn't want me there and expected someone else.

Darya took a moment and sipped her water. Then she said, "Hello, Michael, what a surprise."

I said, "Do you mind if I join you? Are you waiting for someone?"

She gave me a flat stare and said, "Why do you ask?"

"Just curious. All cops are curious. I noticed you're quite curious. Are you a cop in Russia? Or a spy? C'mon, you can trust me."

"I've learned I can trust no one."

I shrugged and said, "Too bad. Life's a lot easier with friends."

Darya said, "It's longer if you don't trust friends." She paused. "You're very sharp. I'm used to dealing with FBI bureaucrats. You're not like them at all."

"Flattery won't help you now."

Darya said, "I want this terrorist stopped as much as you do."

"Dead or alive?"

"That's how Russia views all terrorist hunts."

"There's a lot more to this than just hunting for a fugitive." I waited while she seemed to ponder my question and consider whether she could trust me.

Finally, Darya said, "Are there factions within the NYPD?"

"Yes. All agencies have factions."

"So do we. I suspected it was the same everywhere. Some in my government have different ideas about the war on terror. Unfortunately, they've acted on them. You might call them cowboys or rogues."

"What kind of different ideas do these factions have?"

She brought those intense, blue eyes to rest on me. "We all have the same goal: stop terrorism. Some people in the Russian government feel like the US has not participated the way it should."

I couldn't hide my shock. "Are you saying this is a Russian government–sanctioned attack?"

Darya stayed calm and steady. She didn't rush what she had to say. That was the mark of a pro.

She said, "No, just the opposite. Now this is all hypothetical, of course. But suppose a rogue element, which was now neutralized, had forced a Russian agent to carry out an attack like this."

"Temir Marat worked for the Russian government?"

She lifted her hands and said, "I was just giving you a theory.

I'm doing this because I know you're actually trying to help things."

I said, "I want to capture Temir Marat and question him. What do you want?"

Darya gave no answer.

Before I could press her on it, I glanced up. There, near the front door, at the end of the bar, stood Temir Marat.

CHAPTER 28

IT FELT UNREAL to have been searching for someone so hard and then see him in person not far away. I guess part of me thought Lewis Vineyard was full of shit.

I stared at Marat. A bandage on his cheek covered the cut I'd given him with the bottle. He wore a NY Rangers baseball cap pulled low. He was gazing around the room, looking for someone. I suspected I knew who.

I eased out of my chair, getting ready to make a casual stroll across the dining room to get next to him.

Then I saw the couple coming into the bar behind Marat. A tall, burly man with short hair, and a woman nearly six feet tall with black hair. The man's birthmark told me exactly who he was. The birthmark looked like a smeared tattoo of a purple house.

All I could think was that the FBI was going to owe Lewis Vineyard a truckload of cash.

If I wanted Marat alive, I would have to act quickly.

Then the mob hitters made their move. It was smooth and professional—if I didn't know what I was looking for, I might've missed it.

The man stepped up right next to Temir Marat, folded his hands across his waist, and casually slipped his right hand under his dark linen coat.

It was subtle, but not too subtle. Marat immediately picked up on the man right next to him. He moved like a cat.

I could clearly see the Russian mobster as he pulled his blue steel SIG Sauer P220 semiautomatic pistol. It was an ugly thing, out of place in a nice restaurant like this.

But Marat was smooth as he turned and used both hands to block the gun before it could come up. He locked the man in close, with the pistol pointing almost straight at the floor.

The killer struggled with the gun under the power of Marat's grip. I could tell he was also struggling with the shock. He'd thought this would be easy.

Marat head-butted him, then ripped the gun right out of his hands. Now the woman got involved, reaching into her Louis Vuitton purse to pull out an identical pistol.

Marat reacted immediately, jerking the dazed man right in front of him as the woman pulled the trigger, shooting her partner twice in the chest.

Marat shoved the motionless man toward the woman. The dead weight knocked her off balance.

This all happened before I could even reach the bar. Everyone was looking around, startled by the two gunshots. The echo had made it difficult to pinpoint. This guy really did have skills.

I was a few feet away from the bar when the female hitter regained her balance and had Marat in the corner. The man with the two bullet holes in his chest was dead on the white tile floor. His blood was swirling into dark red pools and running along the grout lines.

Marat didn't have his pistol up yet. He was at the mercy of the female hitter.

I kept coming full speed and threw my entire body into the hitter. It was just a gut reaction.

We both hit the tile hard, but I landed on top of her.

She was out cold, the pistol loose on the floor.

Marat gave me a faint smile, raised the pistol to his forehead, and saluted me before disappearing out the door.

Darya appeared at my side as I was kneeling to make sure the woman was breathing properly.

I said, "Watch her." Then I was on my feet and out the door.

As soon as I hit the open area beyond the restaurant, I had my head on a swivel. There weren't many people out. Then I caught just a glimpse of someone running. It was the way his head bobbed up and down, and the blue and red of the Rangers cap.

He was running south, along the water. I drew my Glock and started to run the same direction. I fell into a measured pace, not knowing what I might have to deal with once I caught this unusual suspect. At least he wouldn't surprise me with his abilities this time.

The park was flat and relatively empty as it got closer to the street. I would see him if he moved away from the water.

Just as I paused by a cement column that depicted the construction of the World Trade Center, I heard a gunshot. The bullet pinged above my head on the column.

Great. Now this was a gunfight.

CHAPTER 29

I CROUCHED ON the other side of the column and brought my pistol up. There were several low concrete shapes in the park designed to be artistic and give people a place to sit and rest.

I crouched low and ran to the first of the cement structures. It wasn't until I dropped behind it that I realized Marat was just beyond, crouching behind a closed food kiosk.

I leaned from behind the cover and popped off two quick rounds, hoping to scare him out of his position. Instead, I was met with two quick rounds back at me.

I knew the gunfire had to attract attention and if I could just hold him in place, help would be on its way soon. But I still wanted to take this guy alive. A patrol officer rolling up on a gunfight wasn't going to take that kind of care. I wouldn't blame any officer that fired a weapon in this situation.

I popped around the edge and fired twice more. Just to let him know I was here and I wasn't giving up. That's when he used his skills once again. Most people, when they are being shot at, will find cover and stay there. Marat started to move as soon as

I fired the two shots. He came low and fast from his cover along the edge of the cement block I was behind.

Next thing I knew, he was right in front of me. I turned and raised my pistol, but he had already twisted and slapped it hard. Then his foot came off the ground in a blur and struck me in the side of the head. I was dazed as I pitched over.

But he didn't want to fight. He just wanted me to stop shooting. He turned and sprinted away toward a series of decorative concrete walls designed to block the wind and give people something to look at. It looked like a tiny maze.

Once again, after I cleared my head, I was running after him as quickly as I could.

I slowed as I came to the walls. I had my pistol up and scanned the whole area, hoping to get a glimpse of Marat. I entered the little maze carefully.

As I came to the last wall, expecting to see Marat in the wide-open space between here and the Clipper City Tall Ship anchored in the water, I spotted some movement out of the corner of my right eye. Just a blur.

Unfortunately, the movement was Marat's fist as it connected with the side of my head. I had to look like a cartoon character with my face twisting under Marat's fist, my eyes spinning, as I tried to protect myself. I thought I was losing consciousness as I dropped my gun and heard it clatter against the rough cement. Then I steadied myself as I bounced off one of the six-foot-high concrete walls.

Marat was on me in an instant.

He threw his whole body into mine, knocking me flat on the ground. Then he picked up my pistol and flung it hard toward the river.

Marat said, "Just stay here. I still have a pistol." He held up the SIG Sauer like I needed some kind of visual cue.

Now he was jogging away again. He thought he had disarmed me. That was his mistake.

CHAPTER 30

I HATE TO admit that I sat on the hard cement for a few seconds just to gather my wits. This guy could've killed me several times over. Why hadn't he?

Now I had an advantage. He thought I was unarmed. I reached down and drew the Smith & Wesson model 36 revolver. I wasn't crazy about going up against a man armed with a .45-caliber semiautomatic while I just had a five-shot .38, but there was no way I could let this guy disappear.

I knew he'd been headed south, so I got to my feet and started to jog unsteadily toward the masts of the Clipper City Tall Ship I could see in the distance.

It was cold and dark, so there were few people in the park or near the ship. I spotted his Rangers cap about halfway between me and the ship. He was walking fast, trying not to draw attention to himself. I knew he was trying to get out of the area. That's what I'd do.

As I closed the distance, I suddenly felt like the .38 in my hand was a BB gun. Where the hell was my backup?

I scanned for cover to get behind before I shouted for him to stop. A drop of blood from a cut on my forehead slipped into my eye. I felt like I'd been run over by a Volkswagen.

The best cover I could find was a heavy, freestanding billboard that advertised tours out of the mouth of the Hudson. I stood behind it, raised my revolver, and sighted from the groove near the gun's hammer to the front sight, with Temir Marat's body taking up my entire sight picture.

I shouted, "Police—don't move!"

He froze.

I spoke loudly and enunciated carefully. "Put the gun on the seawall!" He was right next to the low wall with the open water beyond it. If he tried anything, he had to pull the gun, turn this direction, and then find me in a split second. I liked my position.

Marat just stood there, facing the water. I could still see his hands hanging at his side. There was no telling what a man like this was thinking or how far he'd go.

I shouted again, "Put your pistol on the seawall!" I waited a moment and added, "Do it now."

He never moved his hands as he stepped up onto the seawall and spun to face me. This is not what I wanted to happen. I didn't want him to have a chance to survey the area and see where I was standing. But I didn't feel I could pull the trigger when I saw both of his hands clearly, and didn't see the gun at all.

He glanced over his right shoulder as if he were thinking about jumping in the river. It wouldn't be the first time a suspect tried it. Most people overestimated their swimming ability.

I shouted, "Don't do it, Temir!"

That caught his attention. He just stared at me.

"That's right, I know your name. I know everything about you. I even visited your aunt and uncle in Weequahic. Aunt Vera and Uncle Konstantin."

He was listening. It was a nice change from him punching me.

I stepped out from behind the sign and started to walk slowly toward him. My pistol was still up as I said, "You didn't attack the parade because of a jihad. You're not even Muslim. You're Russian Orthodox like the rest of your family."

Now I was only about ten feet from the seawall. After what this guy had done to me in two different fights, I wasn't about to get any closer.

I was careful how I phrased my next statement. "I think I know who you're working for. We can protect you. All you have to do is surrender."

His right hand twitched and eased toward his jacket's front pocket.

I said, "Don't do it."

The hand froze about halfway to the pocket.

"Surrender and we can work this out."

Then Marat spoke. His voice was even and he clearly had an accent, but his English was good. "If I surrender, you can ignore the people I killed?"

I just stared at him for a moment. I had no answer.

Marat said, "Neither can I." His voice had a catch in it. "I had to do it. They have my wife and daughter."

"Is that why you said *hawqala?*"

"I didn't know if anyone would pick up on it."

I kept the pistol trained on him. I was still expecting someone to come help me shortly.

Marat said, "They told me I had to do this one job. Drive the truck into the parade, then detonate the explosive they had built into the truck. That was my first clue they'd abandoned me. When I hit the detonator, it was supposed to give me thirty seconds to escape. Then there was no one waiting to drive me away like they were supposed to. They've been trying to kill me ever since. Now it looks like they tricked you into doing their dirty work."

All I could say was, "Who? Who is trying to kill you? Who do you work for?"

He looked like he wanted to tell me. Like he knew it was over. He started to speak, then hesitated.

His right hand moved. That's when I heard two gunshots.

CHAPTER 31

AS SOON AS I heard the shots, I couldn't keep from turning to see where they came from. Behind me, partially hidden by a wooden bench, Darya Kuznetsova kneeled with the other Russian mob hitter's pistol in her hand.

I spun back to Marat. He seemed to be frozen. Somehow, in that split second, his right hand had reached the gun in his jacket pocket. Now he held it loosely with the barrel pointed to the ground.

He looked at me and tried to speak. That's when I noticed the two red stains expanding on the front of his jacket. Both were close to his heart.

The pistol dropped onto the seawall. Marat stood for a second longer, then toppled over into the river.

I raced to the seawall and leaned over to look at the dark water. The tide was going out and there was a serious current. But there was no sign of Temir Marat. The swirling black water would hide anything more than a few inches below the surface.

Darya joined me at the seawall. She carefully placed the pistol next to the one that had dropped out of Marat's hand.

I looked at her and simply said, "Why?"

"I thought he was going to shoot you. You have no idea what men like that are capable of."

"I'm starting to get an idea."

"He would've shot you."

I said, "That's bullshit. He's one of yours. You're just trying to cover his tracks."

Darya shook her head and said, "He's not one of mine. I had nothing to do with anything this man was involved in." She was convincing. Then she said, "And I really thought your life was in danger."

Two patrol cars pulled up to the edge of the park and the four patrol officers started jogging toward us with their weapons drawn.

I immediately set down my revolver, pulled my badge from my back pocket and held it in my right hand. To be on the safe side, both of my hands were above my head before they got too close.

Darya took my lead and raised her hands as well.

A female patrol officer who was leading the pack charging toward us recognized me. "Do you need a hand, Detective Bennett?"

Immediately, I felt relief wash through me.

It was over. Maybe not the way I wanted it to end, but the manhunt for Temir Marat was finished.

CHAPTER 32

TWO HOURS LATER, I was sitting on the same seawall where Temir Marat stood when he was shot. My feet dangled over the seawall as I watched the search for Marat's body.

A crime scene was set up where Marat had been shot. The three pistols, mine and the two mobsters' SIG Sauers, were still sitting in the same place on the seawall.

Several harbor boats, two NYPD boats, and the Coast Guard rescue ship were shining lights and casting nets into the murky water.

Someone sat down next to me, and I was surprised when I turned my head to see that it was Dan Santos.

He just sat there watching the water with me for about half a minute. Neither of us said a word.

Finally, I said, "How did your interview with Darya go?"

Santos said, "About how you'd expect. She claims she followed you from the restaurant to help you catch Marat. She picked up a pistol from the floor of the restaurant that came from one of the people trying to kill our suspect. When she found you facing Marat, she thought he was about to shoot you so she fired first."

"But did she say anything about Marat's motive or who he worked for?"

"C'mon, Bennett, give the FBI some credit. As soon as we figured out how *hawqala* had been used in other bombings, and consulted some counterparts at the CIA, we had a pretty good idea what was going on."

"Did you suspect what Darya was up to while she was working with us? I mean, she never intended for us to get our hands on Marat."

Santos smiled and said, "Did you ever see me do, or say, anything classified in front of her?"

I said, "Maybe you're not the dumbass prick I thought you were."

Santos laughed and said, "Once again you're underestimating the FBI. I'm not a dumbass, but I am a prick. Sometimes you have to be in this line of work. Especially when you deal with the NYPD every day."

The only answer I had to that was, "Touché."

CHAPTER 33

I'LL ADMIT TO being a little uncomfortable when Darya asked me to grab a cup of coffee after we were released from the shooting scene. But curiosity got the better of me and I agreed to slip into a coffee shop right at the edge of the financial district.

We sat in silence as I made a show of stirring my coffee until she finally said, "I have no idea why it is important to me that you know I had nothing to do with the attack."

I just nodded. My grandfather had taught me that running your mouth without thought is always a bad idea. When I was a kid I believed he followed all of his own advice.

Darya said, "There is nothing about this incident that I agreed with. I shouldn't even have to say that I'm against terrorism. I'm against any government trying to trick other governments. And I was against the way my government chose to handle the whole situation. And if you repeat anything I say here, I'll simply deny it. I just felt like you had earned an explanation."

"And you didn't want me to think you were a cold-blooded killer."

She shrugged and said, "Frankly, I prefer you think I'm a killer than a liar."

I stared at her, trying to get a feel for her sincerity. She really was striking with those deep-blue eyes and high cheekbones. No matter how I focused, I couldn't get a clear read on her.

Darya said, "I'm pretty certain Dan Santos will never deal with me again, but I would love to hear who hired the two Russian mobsters and tipped them off that I had arranged a meeting with Temir through a mutual acquaintance. If you were able to talk to the woman who survived, is that something you might be able to find out for me?"

I just smiled. There was no way I was going to commit to helping her on anything until I knew more about what had happened during the investigation. I was in a weird no-man's land between the FBI and an official envoy from Russia.

I drank about half my coffee as we sat there and watched the few people on the streets at this time of the night.

Finally, I asked the one question that had been on my mind. "Will the US see any other fake attacks?"

"Not from Russia. Who knows what others have in mind. It's too easy to bend public opinion. Why should a government make a good-faith effort to do the right thing about terrorism or any other hot-button issue, when one incident like the attack on the parade will galvanize the population?"

"What about you? Are you going to stay in New York?"

"For a while. I like it here. I'm starting to understand American police politics and I am certain there will be more incidents where we all have to cooperate."

"I'm afraid of the same thing."

Darya surprised me when she reached across the small table and grasped both of my hands. "I am your friend, Michael. In time, I hope you learn to trust me. I think we could each help the other in a number of ways."

I couldn't deny the logic, but wasn't sure I grasped her entire meaning.

She released my hands and stood up. I immediately stood as well. She stepped toward me, rose up on her tiptoes, and kissed me on the cheek. Then she whispered in my ear, "We'll meet again."

Then she was gone.

CHAPTER 34

THREE NIGHTS AFTER Temir Marat was killed, I sat in the only safe place I knew in the entire world. In my living room with Mary Catherine, nine of my kids, and my grandfather.

Mary Catherine was snuggled in next to me on the couch, with Chrissy and Shawna tucked in on the other side of me. The older kids all sat on the carpet as we watched the Jets on Thursday Night Football. It was a game against the Dolphins in Miami and every camera shot between commercials showed people walking along the beach in shorts. It just didn't feel right to a New Yorker.

Before the game, I had watched the news, where everyone was reporting the attack on the parade as just another terror incident. They went on to say the terrorist was shot by "authorities." Reporters made it a point to say the suspect acted alone.

That seemed to put an end to the terror attack that had rocked the city. Even Ricky said, "So you solved another one, huh, Dad?"

"*Solve* isn't the word I'd use. We *cleared* the case. That'll have to do."

Eddie said, "It's got people on their guard now."

I smiled. "For now, but people forget. Always. It's got to be one of the fundamental laws of the universe."

Mary Catherine said, "You really think the attack will be forgotten?"

"Not totally, but no one will think twice about next year's parade. That's how these things always go. People talk about never forgetting, but they forget remarkably fast. The Freedom Tower is a good reminder, but you have to be in lower Manhattan to see it."

Shawna looked up at me. "We'll still go to the parade next year, won't we?"

Jane chimed in. "We have to, otherwise the terrorists win."

I didn't know if she was serious or joking.

Shawna still stared up at me. "Can we go?"

I smiled. "Of course we'll go. That's our thing. Your mom loved it. In a way, we're honoring her memory. St. Patrick's and Macy's are two parades we won't ever miss."

There were smiles and cheers all around. Mary Catherine hugged me, then kissed me on the lips.

STUCK BETWEEN TWO CARTELS IN A DESPERATE, BLOODY STRUGGLE FOR TERRITORY, MICHAEL BENNETT IS ON EVERYONE'S HIT LIST.

A New York City cop as seasoned as Michael Bennett thinks that nothing can catch him off guard. But then a gorgeous, wealthy woman from South America posing as a photographer lures Bennett into a trap unlike anything he's ever seen—nearly costing him his life. It's up to Bennett to discover the true identity of his adversary before the ambush engulfs him.

READ ON FOR A SNEAK PEEK AT THE UPCOMING MICHAEL BENNETT NOVEL,

AMBUSH

CHAPTER 1

I WATCHED THE eight-story apartment building on 161st, about half a block from Melrose Avenue. Nothing special about it. Old window air-conditioning units dotted the facade, but the place had a certain charm. Of course, over years of surveillance in unsavory neighborhoods of New York City, I've learned to adjust my expectations.

My partner, Antrole Martens, and I were sitting in his Crown Victoria. By tradition, the most beat-up car in our homicide unit went to the rookie on the squad. Despite the faint odor of vomit, Antrole had handled the assignment of the shitty car with grace in his six years with the NYPD. He understood he had to earn his place in the unit, but there was no doubt he was on his way up. I thought he was exactly the kind of cop we needed in a command position.

I wanted this arrest to go well for him. I could still remember my first arrest in homicide. A pimp named Hermine Paschual. He'd stabbed a john who argued about the price. At the time, I thought I was changing the world.

Now it was my job to make sure things went right. I said, "How sure are you about this tip?"

He smiled. "Sure enough to drag your ass out here with me."

"Let your kids get a little older, and life get a little busier, and we'll see how serious you take anonymous tips."

Antrole laughed. "That's why I'm stopping at two kids. Thinking of you managing ten makes my head spin."

"Imagine what it does to me." Just then, my phone rang and I looked down to see that it was my oldest girl, Juliana. I always answered the phone the same way when one of my daughters called.

"Hello, beautiful."

"Hey, Dad!"

There was no teenage disdain today. She was excited about something.

"What's going on, sweetheart?"

"I've got big news. But I have to tell you in person."

"How about at dinner tonight?" I smiled when I heard her giggle. She was not a giggler by nature, so this had to be something good. Harvard flashed in my brain. Although I would've preferred Columbia, a few blocks from our apartment on the Upper West Side.

Juliana said, "I can't wait. I'll tell the whole family at once. I gotta go. Bye, Dad. Love you."

Before I could even say "Love you" back, the connection was dead.

Antrole deadpanned, "Can we squeeze some police work in now? After all, this tip was called in to you. I just happened to answer the phone at your desk."

"Let's call Alice and Chuck to come with us. Maybe Harry, too."

Antrole said, "Why the party? We can grab this dope ourselves. We get all the glory and it'll be easier to talk to him."

"He's a suspect in a murder."

"And we're NYPD detectives. I thought in the old days you guys used to make arrests by yourselves."

"Yeah, we also used to get shot more frequently."

"Am I going to have to shame you into coming with me? Besides, if we have a few minutes alone with this guy, who knows what he'll tell us."

"I hate it when rookies make sense. Let's go." His excitement was contagious.

CHAPTER 2

EVERYONE OUT IN the neighborhood made us for cops as soon as we started walking down the sidewalk. It wasn't as if we were working undercover, but a young black guy in a sharp suit and an older white guy with a sport coat to cover his gun—we could've been in uniform and not been any more obvious.

Our suspect had shot a customer who stiffed him on a bag of heroin, in front of a grocery store in Midtown with plenty of witnesses. A poor business plan all around.

The tip said the suspect was in apartment 416. I didn't trust the elevator to make it up all four floors without some sort of issue, so despite Antrole's objections, we took the stairs. It gave me a minute to talk to my headstrong partner.

I said, "Nothing fancy. We knock and hope he answers. Maybe we try the door to see if it's locked. Otherwise, we come up with another plan that may or may not involve the SWAT team. Got it?"

Antrole nodded.

At each landing, I took a moment to get a feel for the surroundings. Antrole probably thought I needed to catch my breath, but this climb was nothing compared to the basketball games I played with my kids. I took it slow because every apartment building had its own aura. Sometimes it was because of the tenants and sometimes it was because of the area. Either could kill you if you weren't careful.

On the fourth landing, I said, "You ready for this? It doesn't matter what happens, you've done a good job getting us this far. Now we have to use our heads."

"You don't have to talk to me like I'm some kid out of the academy. I have four years' patrol experience and two years in the detective bureau. I'm only new to homicide. Homicide detectives are not the only ones that make arrests."

"I don't *have* to talk to you like that, but I enjoy it. That's one of the advantages of being senior."

I appreciated the smile that spread across Antrole's face. Feeling out a new partner is always an ongoing process, but this guy was all right.

He said, "This suspect might be the key to some of the unsolved homicides connected to the heroin dealers up this way."

"Could be." Antrole was looking at the big picture—rare with new homicide detectives. It showed a ton of promise.

The fourth-floor hallway was empty. That was always good. I paused at the stairwell and just listened to the sounds of the apartment building for almost a full minute. Nothing unusual. Latin music from one apartment. Someone talking loud in another.

As we carefully made our way down the hallway, I heard a TV playing a daytime talk show loudly in another apartment.

The cheap carpet was uneven over a wooden floor that broadcast sound. A wide set of windows at the end of the hallway took the edge off the gloomy vibe of the building.

Then we found ourselves in front of apartment 416. Antrole slipped to the other side of the door and drew his Glock service weapon. I pulled my pistol, too, though I thought it was a little premature.

We listened to the door and I put my hand against it to see if I could feel any vibration. Unexpectedly, it pushed open a few inches.

I looked to Antrole, who angled his head to see into the apartment.

That was odd. Drug dealers in this neighborhood rarely left their doors unbolted, let alone open. It was nice to catch a break once in a while.

From my angle, I could see the suspect we were looking for sitting on a couch under a wide, dirty window. His head leaned back on the rear of the couch. He wasn't moving. I motioned to Antrole that I saw someone inside.

The young detective nodded and turned before I could tell him to wait.

A shadow passed the open door, and I heard someone inside. It was a single word. Some kind of command. I wasn't even sure what language it was. But the subsequent gunfire was unmistakable.

The door appeared to explode and Antrole jumped to the other side of the doorway, his gun up.

I crouched quickly and fired a couple of rounds into the apartment. I didn't see a target; it was just to keep the shooters behind cover. We had to move and move quickly.

The gunfire didn't slow down.

This was an ambush.

CHAPTER 3

ALEXANDRA "ALEX" MARTINEZ aimed her Canon EOS-5D Mark III Digital SLR camera at the tallest of the three young men, who were dressed only in tight white underwear. The abs of all three looked like ice trays and their arms had just enough meat. But the tallest of the three, Chaz, was special. The camera loved Chaz.

Alex realized she was barking at the model next to Chaz when he got too close. It was like having a Matt Groening character pop up in a Renoir.

The top of this building in the Morrisania neighborhood in the Bronx provided an interesting urban backdrop, and conveniently put her in position for another assignment. Photographing nearly naked models was fun, but it didn't pay the bills.

This wasn't a coincidence. Alex had planned the photo session to the last detail, including the location. Just like she did everything else.

She checked her watch. They'd been at it for more than two hours, but she could wrap it up just about any time she wanted.

That was the advantage of being prepared: you usually got the shots you needed quickly.

Then she heard it. A couple of pops, seeming to come from the next block.

The models craned their necks, looked over the side of the building in the direction of the sound. She could look down on 161st Street and see the front of the building the gunfire was coming from.

She turned away from her crew as a smile crept onto her face. It was even more gunfire than she'd anticipated. Michael Bennett had been executed.

CHAPTER 4

ANTROLE AND I crouched low. Gunfire had a way of triggering the instinct to ball up as small as possible. The ambushers kept firing high, as if they expected us to still be standing. It was a classic mistake. The holes along the door and the wall gave me an idea of where the shooters were in the room.

Both Antrole and I started to return fire with our Glocks. The shooters had lost the element of surprise and our police training and tactics gave us the upper hand now. I saw a shadow move near the door and peppered it with .40-caliber rounds. Splinters and debris filled the open doorway.

A bullet pinged off a metal doorframe across from me. It struck a Pokémon sticker between the eyes. I hoped the shooter wasn't good enough to have aimed for it.

A splinter the size of a toothpick lodged in my left hand. Pain shot up my arm and blood spread across my fingers.

Now I could hear the shouts and cries from people in the other apartments, which distracted me from whoever was shooting at us. But only for a moment. A door opened a crack and a head popped out. All I could see was gray hair.

Antrole shouted, "Police—get back inside!"

Someone yanked the old man back into the apartment.

Antrole backed against the far wall of the hallway and scooted to my side of the door, just as a wave of shots hit where he had been crouched. Shouting at the civilian had given away his position.

He hunkered down next to me with his pistol up and I felt the tide turning. All we had to do was move down the hallway and wait for the cavalry to arrive. 911 calls had to be flooding in about now. Time was on our side.

Then a shotgun blast blew a hand-size hole just above my head. Jesus Christ. It felt like a bazooka. I choked on some of the drywall dust launched into the air and blinked to clear it out of my eyes. Sweat gathered on my forehead and I felt myself pant.

The shotgun racked on the other side of the wall. The shooter would fire again at any second.

Antrole yelled, "Clip!"

He was reloading so I needed to keep my gun up. Our training would save us.

I saw a shadow pass the hole in the wall where the shotgun had done its work, and fired twice as Antrole opened up on the doorway again. Someone hit the floor hard on the other side of the wall.

Bullets hit the wall all around us after Antrole fired. He stumbled awkwardly onto the floor.

I looked down and saw that Antrole had been hit in the leg. Blood was pumping out onto the cheap carpet, making the washed-out colors in the fabric come alive with red.

I leaned in close and said, "Can you walk?"

"If it will get us away from here, hell yes."

It felt like maybe the gunfight was over. No one was shooting, a welcome change.

Something flew out of the door and bounced back off the wall. It made an odd thumping sound on the floor right in front of the door. I saw it roll around in odd arcs on the ground.

Too late, I realized it was a hand grenade.

CHAPTER 5

MY EYES FOCUSED on the old-style army pineapple grenade, almost hypnotized.

Out of instinct, I reached down and grabbed Antrole by the collar. He raised his pistol and fired at whoever had tossed the hand grenade from the other side of the door. It was tough pulling 180 pounds across the rough, cheap carpet, a lesson in physics and friction.

I couldn't tell how many shooters were left inside the apartment, but Antrole was laying down fire to keep their heads down. At least one of them was still active. I could hear him scuttling around the apartment, then he fired a round through the wall.

Someone at the other end of the hallway popped out of their apartment and started to run. A young man in a white T-shirt disappeared down the stairwell. It distracted the shooter in the apartment, too. For an instant, everything went quiet.

When I had dragged Antrole a few feet down the hallway, his collar gave way and ripped completely from his coat. I tumbled backward onto the floor and felt a sting of pain, a finger on my left hand turned awkwardly. I desperately reached out to grab my partner again. It felt like I had dropped him down a well. I shouted something, but by now my ears were ringing so badly I don't even know what I said.

That's when it happened. The grenade detonated.

A giant wave of light and heat. I don't know that I'd ever experienced anything close to it. I couldn't even say it made a sound, my ears shut down so fast.

I felt pain on my forehead, but only for a moment.

Then everything went cloudy.

Then it went dark.

AMBUSH

AVAILABLE OCTOBER 2018

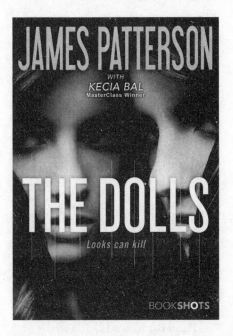

TWO BODIES ARRIVED AT THE MORGUE—AND ONE WAS STILL BREATHING.

A wealthy woman checks into a hotel room and entertains a man who is not her husband. A shooter blows away the lover and wounds this millionairess, leaving her for dead. Is it the perfect case for the Women's Murder Club—or just the most twisted?

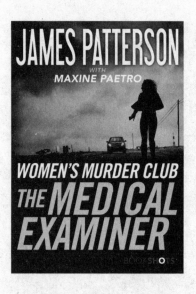

MONEY. BETRAYAL. MURDER.
THAT'S A *PRIVATE* CONVERSATION.

Hired to protect a visiting American woman, Private Johannesburg's Joey Montague is hoping for a routine job looking after a nervous tourist. After the apparent suicide of his business partner, he can't handle much more. But this case is not what it seems—and neither is his partner's death.

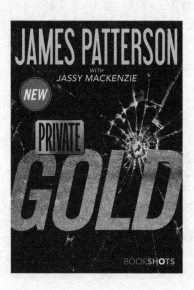

Read the thrilling new addition to the Private series,
Private: Gold, **available only from**

BOOK**SHOTS**

DR. CROSS, THE SUSPECT IS YOUR PATIENT.

An anonymous caller has promised to set off deadly bombs in Washington, DC. A cruel hoax or the real deal? By the time Alex Cross and his wife, Bree Stone, uncover the chilling truth, it may already be too late....

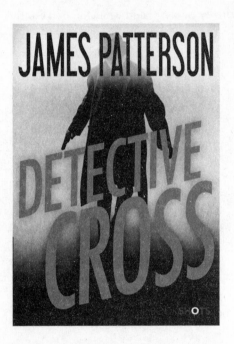

Read the new addition to the Alex Cross series,
Detective Cross, **available only from**

BOOKSHOTS

BONJOUR, DETECTIVE LUC MONCRIEF.
NOW WATCH YOUR BACK.

Very handsome and charming French detective Luc Moncrief
joined the NYPD for a fresh start—but someone wants to make
his first big case his last.

Welcome to New York.

  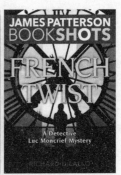

**Read all of the heart-pounding thrillers in the
Luc Moncrief series:**

French Kiss
The Christmas Mystery
French Twist

Available only from

BOOK**SHOTS**

HE'S WORTH MILLIONS...
BUT HE'S WORTHLESS WITHOUT HER.

Siobhan Dempsey came to New York with a purpose: she wants to become a successful artist. But then she meets tech billionaire Derick Miller, who takes her breath away. And though Siobhan's body comes alive at his touch, their relationship has been a roller-coaster ride.

Are they meant to be together?

Read the steamy Diamond Trilogy books:

Dazzling, The Diamond Trilogy: Book I
Radiant, The Diamond Trilogy: Book II
Exquisite, The Diamond Trilogy: Book III

Available only from